Red Sand, Blue Sky

A Clear Spring
by Barbara Wilson

Red Sand, Blue Sky
by Cathy Applegate

Red Sand, Blue Sky

Cathy Applegate

THE FEMINIST PRESS
AT THE CITY UNIVERSITY OF NEW YORK
FEMINISTPRESS.ORG

Published by the Feminist Press at the City University of New York
The Graduate Center, 365 Fifth Avenue, Suite 5406
New York, New York 10016
feministpress.org

First Feminist Press edition, 2002
Originally published in 1995 by Margaret Hamilton Books Pty Ltd, A
Division of Scholastic Australia Pty Ltd, Sydney, Australia.

Library of Congress Cataloging-in-Publication Data

Applegate, Cathy.
  Red sand, blue sky / Cathy Applegate.— 1st Feminist Press ed.
    p. cm. — (Girls first!)
  Summary: When twelve-year-old Amy goes to visit her Auntie Caroline,
a nurse living in a community near Alice Springs, Australia, she and an
Aboriginal girl become friends and help out during an emergency.
  ISBN 1-55861-278-5 (alk. paper)
  1. Australian aborigines—Juvenile fiction. [Australian aborigines—
Fiction. 2 Racism—Fiction. 3. Friendship—Fiction. 4. Aunts—Fiction.
5. Alice Springs (N.T.)—Fiction 6. Australia—Fiction.] I. Title. II. Series

PZ7.A6482 Re 2002
[Fic]—dc21

2001054461

The Feminist Press would like to thank Mariam K. Chamberlain,
Johnetta B. Cole, Florence Howe, Joanne Markell, Genevieve Vaughan,
Henny Wenkart, and Patricia Wentworth and Mark Fagan for their gener-
osity in supporting this book.

Cover illustration copyright © 2002 by Karen Ritz
Text design and composition by Dayna Navaro

For my parents, Lesley and Leslie, and for the Aboriginal Health Workers I've worked with over the years

Contents

Australia

Note to Readers

The story you are about to read takes place in the out-back of Australia, in a small town near Alice Springs where many of the people are Aboriginal. Australia is an island continent that lies between the Pacific and Indian Oceans, some 7,000 miles west of the United States. It was first inhabited by people who walked or sailed from Asia 65,000 years ago. Today known as Aborigines (this word means "from the beginning"), they lived mostly along the coasts, where they moved from place to place following the animals they hunted and the seasonal plants they picked for food.

When the British arrived in 1788 to establish a colony in Australia, there were about 500 Aboriginal tribes, each with its own language and customs. Over time, the white settlers drove the Aborigines away from the coasts, where the land is fertile, and into the out-back, which is desert. Sometimes the settlers used violent means to remove the Aborigines. Later the new government passed laws that denied land rights to Aborigines and made it possible to take Aboriginal children from their parents.

Although the outback is dry and harsh, the Aborigines had explored it from earliest times. In some tribes, when boys reached the age of manhood, they were sent on a "walkabout." This required them to survive alone in the outback and find their way home. Each tribe that traveled through the outback gathered stories about the spirits believed to live in the rock formations of the desert or to appear as kangaroos and other animals. These stories, which tell of the earth's creation, are called dreamings because they are experienced as visions and voices. As a tribe member learns the landscape of the outback, he or she forms bonds with certain places or animals, and can then see or hear their spirits. Some places in the outback are considered sacred for this reason.

Today the outback continues to be home to many of Australia's Aboriginal people. Although some live in Alice Springs, or in coastal cities, many retain their connection to the natural landscape and to the customs of their ancestors.

1
Brighton Beach

It was one of those very still afternoons that are typical of Melbourne in midsummer. Amy could see a number of yachts struggling to get home across Port Phillip Bay. Seagulls wheeled above in the blueness of a clear sky.

On the beach, families were shaking sand off towels and getting ready to leave. Children splashed in the water, playing in the gentle swell. They filled brightly colored buckets with shells and seaweed, ignoring their parents' calls that it was time to go home.

A seagull screeched nearby, loud enough to make Amy jump. She turned and saw that the bird was hopping along beside them as they walked down toward the beach houses.

"They've found us already," she laughed, and clutched the paper package closer, feeling the warmth of the fish and chips through her T-shirt.

"Should we try our usual place?" asked her father.

"Yes, it's nice there," Amy replied with a nod of her head.

They walked past the row of brightly painted shacks that sat amongst the drifts of sand, looking out to sea. At the end of the row, one beach house stood a little apart from the others, as though it didn't quite belong. It rested on stumpy stilts and a small set of weathered steps led up to a closed door.

It was the only hut on the beach that had not received a coat of new paint, and its bleached, pale blue skin was peeling away, revealing cracked timbers. It reminded Amy of a deserted old man keeping watch over the tides.

Amy and her father, Robert, sat down on the top step, backs resting on the door and the paper parcel rustling between them.

Amy loved these times down at the beach. They would sit munching on a takeout dinner, and she would scan the horizon for ships coming into port. The water seemed to stretch on forever as she gazed out to where the bay met the ocean. There was something wonderful about that horizon. It gave her such a strange feeling—something intangible beckoning to her, but always just beyond her reach. She wished sometimes that she could be one of those birds playing in the warm currents of air above. Yes, if she had wings she would fly toward that horizon and never look back, not once.

Amy sighed and reached for her hair, twisting it into one long yellow braid.

"Your friend's caught up with us," her father noted, nodding his head toward the persistent gull. It hopped closer, looked hopefully at the paper package, and tipped its head to one side, fixing them with one alert, humorless eye.

"Doesn't it know that chips are bad for birds?" Amy said as she tore a hole through the paper. The smell was too much for the bird, and it began jumping from one leg to the other, folding and unfolding its wings in tremulous anticipation.

"For goodness' sake," said Robert, "put the poor creature out of its misery." He picked up a chip and threw it to the bird. "Here you go. Amy thinks you should go and get your cholesterol level checked. You're not eating a healthy diet!"

Amy laughed as the grateful bird flew off with the chip held firmly in its beak. "It'll be back," she said. "And no doubt bring its friends as well!"

"Well, let's hurry and get some for ourselves before the starving hoards descend on us," said Robert, offering his daughter another chip.

They ate for a while in silence, watching the waves and the few people left scattered on the beach.

A man jogged past and managed a smile through his gasps for breath. His stomach wobbled up and down violently with each heavy step.

"That'll be you in ten years' time, Dad," laughed Amy.

"Don't say that," groaned Robert in reply. "I feel old enough as it is. And just for that, I'll have another handful of chips."

"Hey, leave some for me!"

"That's what they're saying, too," said Robert, gesturing toward the growing circle of hungry gulls. He threw a chip into the midst of the pack. It erupted in squawks and a great flapping of wings. One gull managed to wrestle the chip away and flew off with a couple of the other birds in hot pursuit.

"So, how was school today, anyway?" Robert asked as he threw a corner of fish to the remaining birds.

"OK."

"OK. Is that all? Can't you elaborate on 'OK'?"

"You always ask me that question, Dad." Amy sighed.

"I know, and for years I've heard the same reply." He shook his head. "You're twelve years old! At least you could make up something to keep your poor old father happy," he added, in a mournful voice.

"Well," said Amy, "if you insist. Actually at school today we were visited by Martians. They landed in the school yard in a silver spaceship and kidnapped Mr. Johnson. They'll probably conduct scientific experiments on him. Hopefully they'll keep him until after the history test next week." Amy stuffed another chip in her mouth triumphantly.

"Goodness." Robert feigned amazement. "I'll have to remember to pack a laser stun gun in with your lunch next week!"

Amy laughed. "If only something like that would really happen."

"Poor Mr. Johnson!"

"Poor me, having to do a stupid history test." Amy took a mouthful of fish. "Anyway, how was your work today?" she asked out of the corner of her rather full mouth.

"OK."

She laughed. "Come on. You'll have to do better than that! No Martians?"

"Definitely not!"

"Very boring. You should come to school with me." Amy was distracted as another jogger puffed past. Down at the water, a small child was crying because he didn't want to go home.

The sun was dipping toward the horizon and the sky

had turned pale pink. Amy could still see the curve of the West Gate Bridge on the other side of the bay and, farther along, the angular silhouette of the city skyscrapers.

There were lots of boats on the water today. There always were at this time of year. Once Amy had even seen an old-fashioned sailing ship. It had made her wonder what it must have been like when the very first tall ships had sailed into this bay nearly two hundred years ago.

"That would have been a real adventure," she thought to herself.

Robert helped himself to the last piece of fish, screwed up the paper wrapper into a tight ball, and wandered over to the nearby trash can with gulls hopping anxiously around his feet.

"Come on," he said. "We'd better be getting home. It's getting late."

Amy and her father had a nice long, roundabout way of walking home from the beach. They walked past the shops, stopping to gaze in the windows, and through the park, and sometimes they took a break to watch people playing tennis at the local club. They were never in a hurry.

Even when they eventually arrived at their street, they'd stop several times along the way to talk over fences with friends.

The only neighbor Amy tried to avoid was old Mrs. Crippen. The poor woman meant well but was quite senile and always got Amy's name wrong. That wouldn't have been such a problem, but the names were always strange and old-fashioned, like Christobel and Beryl. And sometimes her dad would persist in calling her the new name for the rest of the day, which drove her really crazy. He thought it was a huge joke and said that Amy was silly to let it upset her so much.

Halfway down the street, Amy saw that Mrs. Crippen was in her front garden. "Oh, no," she thought. Today she just wanted to be plain old Amy Wilson.

She glanced sideways at her dad, who winked and said, "Why don't you go on ahead. I'll talk to her. She's always got some interesting stories."

Amy didn't need persuading. "See you later, Dad," she mumbled, and heard him laugh as she ran off.

It wasn't far to her front gate. She paused to look into the next-door neighbors' place. They'd just bought a flashy new car and it sat in the driveway—a big, sleek, shining red bullet. The Fullers had lots of money.

Amy opened her gate and grimaced as she caught sight of her father's car, a pink ten-year-old Holden.

Why did it have to be pink? And as if the color wasn't bad enough, it was always filthy dirty—a sort of gray-pink, really. Cleaning wasn't one of her father's strong points.

She sighed, and turned to collect the letters that jutted from the mailbox. She rummaged around for the spare key they kept hidden in a nearby pot plant, and opened the front door.

It was starting to get quite dark, so she turned on a few lights and threw the letters down on the kitchen table before pouring herself a large glass of cold milk from the fridge. The newspaper lay open on the bench, a half-finished crossword staring defiantly up out of the page. She had just flicked through to the comic strips when she heard the gate clang, and knew that her father was home already.

As he came in the front door, the telephone rang and Amy ran to answer it. "It'll be Jenny," she explained, as she picked up the receiver. But it wasn't. In fact, Amy did not recognize the soft, polite, woman's voice on the other end at all.

"It's for you, Dad," she said, as she handed him the phone. "No idea who it is."

From behind the kitchen door, she could hear her father talking. She would never have listened in to his phone conversations in normal circumstances, but something about the voice on the other end of the phone made her very curious, and even a little wary.

Her father sounded funny. His voice was all different and Amy wondered why. He was speaking more softly than usual and she found it difficult to hear complete sentences.

A moment later she heard a good-bye, and with a pang of guilt she rushed to sit at the kitchen table as if she'd been there all the time. She picked up one of the letters and turned it over in her hands, trying to look relaxed and unconcerned.

"Would you like a drink, Amy? Water or juice?" Robert wandered over to the sink and began rinsing out a couple of cups.

"No thank you."

"That was Emma—one of the women at work," he said, without turning around.

Amy tapped the end of the letter up and down on the table sharply. She felt irritated and restless.

"You'll probably meet her sometime soon," her father continued.

"I hope not," thought Amy to herself. "Great," she said out loud. But she made it sound obviously unenthusiastic.

Her father turned and looked at her with a puzzled look on his face.

"Don't be like that, Amy."

"Don't be like what?" She tapped the letter harder and faster.

"You don't have to be so nasty about it. Emma's only a friend." He put the kettle on the stove. "And stop that noise!"

Amy stopped and began twisting the envelope instead. As she turned it over in her hands, the name and address caught her eye. She felt a lump start in her throat.

Mrs. Ruth Wilson. It was unbelievable. When were they ever going to get it right! They shouldn't make mistakes like that. It had been two years now, two years to correct the stupid computers, or whoever it was that addressed these letters.

Amy suddenly felt angry—very angry. She grabbed the letter and wrenched it into two jagged pieces. Throwing it down on the table, she stormed out of the room, up the stairs, and into her bedroom, with her father calling anxiously after her.

Lying on her bed, she wanted to cry, but the tears just wouldn't come. She imagined her father sitting in the kitchen, head in hands, staring at the torn letter. Her head swam with pain and guilt.

If only . . . if only she had wings. Then she would fly far, far away and never look back—not once.

2
The Long Road

It had been over two hours of traveling already, over two hours of bumping and jolting over a red dirt road.

Amy removed a stray wisp of her long hair from the corner of her mouth, but the wind from the open car window soon whipped it around again. She twisted in her seat and faced the window so that the wind blew her hair in a stream behind her. The heat and brightness of the day hit her full in the face and she squinted her blue eyes into two narrow slits.

Sand and scrub! She'd never seen anything like this before in her life—a vast expanse of desert sand just lying in wait for a stray breeze to stir it into life—a sea of sunburned red country dotted with spinifex and mulga, stunted bushes and little old wizened trees. In the distance, the land met the brilliance of the blue sky at a stark horizon.

Amy turned away from the window and rubbed the fine sand out of her eyes.

"I suppose Alice Springs is back there somewhere," she thought with a little sigh. The view through the back window was completely obscured by the dust being thrown up by the car. It billowed up in a great cloud, then hung in the air like a red curtain.

A noise in the car distracted Amy from her thoughts. It was the little baby again, gooing and gurgling in its mother's arms. It looked at Amy and smiled, showing two new white teeth, before turning shyly to bury its head in its mother's hair.

The woman smiled down at the little dark head at her shoulder and said something to the lady beside her. Amy could not hear a word above the noise of the car, but as she watched the woman's lips move, she knew that she would not have understood anyway. These women were not speaking English, but their own Aboriginal language.

Amy turned away and thought how strange it was that she had lived all her life in Australia and never met an Aboriginal person before this day. Who'd have believed that she would find herself as the odd person out. She and her Auntie Caroline were the only white-skinned people in the car.

"This is the strangest day of my life," she thought. "If only Dad could see me now!"

Everything was different! She had never been in a car like this before. It was really more like a small truck. The front seat had room for about four people to sit side by side. The back of the car, where Amy sat, had two long seats along the side walls so that the passengers sat facing each other. The door at the rear of the car was fastened with a latch that was a little loose, rattling and clanking as the vehicle hit bumps and grooves in the road.

Through the front windshield, Amy could see a long, blue radio antenna attached to the hood. A black box with lots of dials and switches was fastened inside the car above the dashboard.

"That must be some sort of radio," she thought.

When Auntie Caroline had collected Amy from the airport, the car had been empty. However, a quick stop at the hospital had changed that. There had been about ten people waiting for a ride back to their hometown in the desert. Amy had soon been sandwiched between two women, with her small backpack pushed up under one of the seats, out of the way.

"You Caroline's niece?" one of the women had asked, with the flash of a bright smile. And Amy had just nodded, feeling a little overwhelmed by the whole situation. The people had talked among themselves until the car left Alice Springs and headed out onto the highway. Sometimes they spoke in English, and sometimes in Luritja, their Aboriginal language. Once the car had picked up speed, the noise of the engine and the rattle of the car's frame made conversation impossible. But nobody seemed to want to talk any more now, turning instead to look out the windows at the passing country and occasionally pointing out sights of apparent interest to their companions.

Amy tried not to stare. She did not wish to appear rude, but found herself fascinated by these people, so different from anyone she had met before.

A man sitting in the corner opposite Amy had a long white cast on his leg.

"I wonder how he hurt himself?" she thought. As she watched, the man pulled a bag out from under the seat and extracted half a barbecued chicken. He pulled off a drumstick and passed the remaining chicken to an old lady sitting to his right. Amy had been studying her before. Never in her life had she seen anyone so old and wrinkled. The woman had a red scarf tied tightly around her forehead, keeping her tousled white hair off her face. Beneath it, two eyes stared unseeing and Amy could see that the central black of each eye had been frosted over white.

"Funny," thought Amy. "I hadn't noticed that lump on her lip before."

From the corner of the old woman's mouth there protruded a large, brown growth. It looked very ugly and Amy wondered why they hadn't removed it for her in hospital.

"You all right back there?" Auntie Caroline had twisted around in the front seat to smile at Amy. Amy nodded, not wanting to yell above the engine noise. "Nearly there," Caroline added.

The car now slowed and there was a rattle as they crossed over a grid in the road, which was there to keep cattle from crossing. A large sign to one side said something about "Entering Aboriginal Land" and "Permits" and "No Alcohol Allowed," but Amy did not get a chance to read the details before the car picked up speed again.

"Nearly there," thought Amy with a smile. "That's what Caroline said over an hour ago!" She sighed and squirmed. The seats were certainly not very comfortable and Amy wished she had a cushion.

Someone handed her a piece of chicken, which she accepted out of politeness. She was beginning to feel a little hungry. And thirsty as well.

She turned to look out the window again, hoping that she might see the beginnings of a town. The wind had whipped her hair around into her mouth again and she spat it out with annoyance. She saw that they were now traveling parallel to a mountain range that loomed out of the desert like the back of a slumbering prehistoric monster. She could almost imagine it getting slowly to its feet and lumbering off toward the horizon.

This mountain range was so different from those she'd seen before in the country north of Melbourne. This was old and worn—worn down by millions of years of wind and rain. Amy suddenly understood what people meant when they said Australia was an old land, and for a moment she felt small and insignificant next to these ancient red giants.

"I wonder what you'd see from the top of one of those mountains?" she mused. "I bet the country just goes on forever and ever."

It was hard to believe that only this morning she'd been sitting safely cocooned in her bedroom in Melbourne. It was hard to believe that this was all part of the same country.

"I wonder if she has ever been to Melbourne?" thought Amy, staring at the old lady again. "Wait a minute!" Amy blinked in amazement. The lump on the woman's lip had disappeared. "That can't be right," thought Amy puzzled. "Am I imagining things now?" She shrugged her shoulders and turned away.

"I wonder how Dad is doing?" she thought, flicking her hair back off her face again. "He should be on his way to Canada by now, and getting nervous about presenting his paper at the conference."

Canada! How she had wanted to go to Canada with her father. But no, he said she'd be bored. He'd be at the conference all day and she'd be stuck in a hotel room for two weeks. Besides, they couldn't afford it.

Amy had not been at all keen about the idea of going to stay with Auntie Caroline way out in the middle of nowhere. But after some thinking, she'd slowly come around to the idea. Amy and Caroline had always been very good friends, and she'd missed her terribly since her aunt had moved from Melbourne to the small Central Australian community. Amy's dad, who was Caroline's big brother, often complained, saying: "I don't know why she had to move and go and live out there, of all places." He'd shake his head. "Wants to save the world or something. Don't know why she couldn't keep working as a nurse at St. Mary's. Now that was a nice little hospital."

The last two years had been such a difficult time for the family. Caroline had helped a lot, and that love and support was missed a great deal since she'd left Melbourne.

"Dad and I have managed somehow without her," thought Amy. "We've stuck it out together—until now." Yes, it had all changed.

Amy's thoughts were interrupted by a change in the engine noise. They were slowing down again and the car gradually came to a stop at an intersection. The woman with the baby was gesturing, pointing out the window at something in the landscape. Amy turned and squinted into the brightness.

"You see it?" the woman asked.

"No," replied Amy, shaking her head.

"Look again," the woman said gently. "Emu . . . in Luritja we say *kalaya* . . . over there. You can see him."

Amy turned back to the window and peered even harder, scanning the country for a large, swift-running bird—for an emu. It was no use. All she could see was red sand and bushes.

"See?" The woman smiled, revealing one front tooth missing. "You see?" she asked again.

"I th-think so . . . , " stammered Amy, anxious not to offend.

The woman said something in Luritja to her friend and they both looked at Amy and laughed gently. The old blind woman cackled loudly.

Amy blushed right to the roots of her blonde hair and turned again to look out the window. Still no emu.

"Don't worry." It was Caroline, who'd overheard the conversation. "You'll get used to it. These people see things in the land that I can never see."

"It seems I've got a lot to get used to," Amy sighed.

The car had turned right at the intersection and the engine noise rose above the conversation once again.

Everyone settled back in the seats, although now Amy noticed a restlessness in their movements. One person started checking his bag and the woman with the baby was smiling and talking to her child. Amy began to get the feeling that maybe the journey was nearing its end at last.

Sure enough, a short time later, she saw some dwellings by the side of the road. They were not houses like her home back in Melbourne. These were more like tents, except they were made out of huge sheets of curved corrugated iron. Amy could see people sitting on the ground around the shelters, occasional smoke from a campfire spiraling into the air.

"I know Auntie Caroline's a little eccentric. I know she likes adventure," thought Amy, a little shakily. "But please, please, don't make me stay in one of those for two weeks. I like camping, but not that much!"

She breathed a secret sigh of relief as a couple of houses came into view. Indeed, as they drove on, they passed about twenty simple houses. They looked strangely out of place. There were no gardens, no lawns or trees anywhere to be seen. Just red sand everywhere.

"That's the police station." Caroline pointed to a large brick building with a high fence all around. "And that's the health clinic over there. That's where I work."

The car stopped outside the clinic building. It was small and slightly run-down. A group of people sat on the ground under a shady veranda.

"Just a quick stop here, Amy," said Caroline over her shoulder. "And then home."

Someone opened the back doors of the car, which swung back, groaning on their hinges. Soon the weary travelers were clambering out to greet waiting friends and relatives.

The Luritja language filled the air and Amy wished she could understand what was being said.

"Do you want a ride home?" Caroline was talking to the young woman with the baby.

The woman nodded quickly in reply and climbed into the front seat.

"You, too, Amy," Caroline said with a smile. "Climb out and come around to the front seat. There's plenty of room."

Soon the car rattled into motion once more.

"We'll just drop Lillian off, and then I'll take you home to my place," Caroline said, as they bumped along. "I'll bet you'd like a cold drink or a cup of tea or both. And a shower, too, I guess." She paused as they turned left onto another of the village's rough dirt roads.

"So what do you think of my new hometown?" she asked, raising one eyebrow and looking sideways at her niece.

"Well," said Amy. "Well, it's certainly different from Melbourne!"

Caroline laughed.

3
Home Sweet Home

Amy stood in front of the bathroom mirror. Her hair was sticking out at all angles, covered with red dust.

"I look like a scarecrow," she murmured to herself.

She fished around in her bag for a comb and, gritting her teeth, began the painful task of untangling her matted hair.

After she'd showered and put on a fresh change of clothes, she brushed her clean hair and tied it into one long tight braid down her back.

"Ah, that's better," said Caroline with a smile, when Amy eventually emerged. "Would you like a drink? The water just boiled if you'd like a cup of tea. Do you still drink tea?"

Amy nodded. "I do. But not very often." When Amy was very small, she had spent a lot of time at

Caroline's house in Melbourne. One of their special games had been tea parties, and her aunt had made her cups of tea that were mainly milk with a dash of hot tea from the teapot. It had made her feel very grown-up. Since then, a cup of tea had become a secret pleasure they shared.

Amy smiled, thinking back to the time when Caroline had lived in Melbourne.

"I'd love some tea," she said, and sat down at a small round table where she could watch her aunt, busy in the small kitchen. Caroline hadn't changed a bit—except for her hair. She'd had it cut very short so that now her head was covered with dark brown curls. But nothing else was different. Amy saw the same vivacious sparkle in Caroline's dark eyes.

"We've only got powdered milk, I'm afraid," Caroline said as she reached for a container on an upper shelf. "No cows to milk out here."

"That's OK," said Amy. "I'm already getting the idea that things are a little different here."

Caroline's house was very small, but comfortable enough. The front door opened into the main living area, which was furnished with three comfortable lounge chairs at one end and the round table, where Amy now sat, at the other. A bench separated the living room from the kitchen.

One door led to a bathroom that also served as a laundry room and another opened to a small bedroom. Caroline had made it quite homey, with a few photos and posters stuck on the white walls. Amy had noticed the cot squeezed between one wall and Caroline's bed, and had placed her backpack neatly under it. Above her bed hung a picture of a Melbourne streetcar cruising down the middle of a busy city street.

"Where's your TV?" asked Amy. "I've got to watch *Country Practice* tonight. It's a really exciting episode."

"There's no television out here, Amy," Caroline laughed. "We're too far away from the main TV stations and we can't get any reception unless we install a satellite dish. I don't even have a telephone," she added, "although I believe the Community Council is thinking of having a few installed soon." She handed Amy a cup of tea.

Amy digested this information in silence, then asked in a small voice, "Do you really like it here?" She couldn't imagine life without a television or a telephone. It didn't seem right at all.

Caroline didn't answer right away. She came and sat down at the table and placed her cup of tea in front of her, grasped in both hands. She gazed thoughtfully out the window.

"Yes, I do like it," she said at last. "But it's certainly not easy. My work is very busy. Sometimes too busy. But it's basically a friendly place and the people have shown me a lot of kindness and taught me a great deal. Of course there are some people here with problems, as there are in any town you could name in Australia."

"What kind of problems?" Amy asked.

"Well, mainly for the young people," replied Caroline, sipping her tea. "I guess a lot of them are bored. There's not much to do in a small town like this once they finish school. One of the biggest problems here is that there are very few jobs. Even if they move to Alice Springs away from their families, there aren't many jobs. So they often end up with nothing to do and it's not much fun just sitting around all day."

"Sounds OK to me," said Amy mischievously.

"Maybe it does," said Caroline with a sad smile, "but Amy, if you had nothing to do, day in, day out, and no challenges, you'd be really miserable in no time at all."

"I guess so," said Amy slowly. "That's what Dad says, too, when he's trying to get me to do my homework."

Caroline's face brightened once again at the mention of Amy's father.

"How is Robert, anyway?" she asked with a smile.

"Busy, as always," Amy replied, sighing a little. "Ever since he started his own business he's had late nights and he brings a lot of work home, too. He gets very tired."

"Yes, he always was one to take on too much," said Caroline with a shake of her head. "He's happy, though?"

"I guess so." Amy paused and took a deep breath. "He's got a girlfriend, you know."

"No, I didn't." Caroline sounded surprised.

"Yes," Amy continued, avoiding Caroline's questioning eyes. "Her name's Emma."

"Is she nice?" asked her aunt, looking at Amy with an amused expression.

"Hmm . . ." mumbled Amy, gazing intently into her cup of tea and wishing that she'd never brought the subject up at all.

"I see," replied Caroline. "So you don't get along very well, I gather."

"It just takes some getting used to, I guess." Amy still avoided her aunt's quizzical eyes.

"I guess it does," replied Caroline softly. "Oh, look at the time. I didn't tell you that Elizabeth, the other nurse who works here, has asked us over for dinner tonight. We're supposed to be there already."

Caroline took a quick shower and changed out of her blue nurse's uniform into a comfortable skirt and T-shirt. She ran a comb quickly through her brown curls and inspected herself briefly in the bathroom mirror. "Let's go," she said.

It was getting dark as Caroline and Amy once again climbed up into the car and drove the short distance to Elizabeth's place.

The smell of roasting meat met them at the front door, and Amy suddenly realized how hungry she felt. It had been a long day.

As they entered, Amy saw that the house was an exact replica of Caroline's. The only difference was in the furniture and the paintings on the walls.

"Hello, you must be Amy," said Elizabeth as she welcomed them inside. She was a plumpish, middle-aged woman with honey brown skin and a smile that put Amy at ease right away.

"Good to see you back, Carol," she said. "It's been very busy. How was your trip to town?"

"Good, Liz. Good," replied Caroline, relaxing into a comfortable chair. "Have a seat, Amy. You'll have to excuse us if we catch up a little and I find out what's been happening at work."

Amy sat down in a chair next to her aunt. She was glad she didn't have to talk. She looked around at all the Aboriginal paintings that Elizabeth had hanging on the walls. The canvases were covered with little dots of paint that swirled in browns, dusky reds, and other colors that reminded her of the surrounding country.

"Yes, the trip was good," Caroline was saying. "We went and picked up the supplies of medicines and bandages, got the car radio fixed at last, and picked up a few people from the hospital. And of course we visited the airport to pick up Amy. We weren't too late, were we?" she asked Amy with a smile.

"I hope you didn't have to wait too long for your auntie, Amy," said Elizabeth. "She's got a habit of being late."

"Only about fifteen minutes, I think," replied Amy politely.

"Now don't you go spreading rumors about me, Liz," said Caroline with a laugh.

They were interrupted by a knock on the door. A tall, slim Aboriginal woman entered and Amy caught her breath, trying not to stare. She had never expected to see an Aboriginal person with blonde hair. But this woman's thick hair was golden, contrasting sharply with the dark brown of her skin.

The woman moved with easy grace to a chair.

"Hello, Barbara," said Caroline. "This is my niece, Amy."

Barbara turned and smiled at Amy.

"Hello," said Amy, hoping that no one had seen her staring.

"You're from Melbourne?" Barbara asked in a deep, quiet voice.

"Yes, I'm here with my auntie for two weeks. Dad's at a conference in Canada," she added by way of explanation.

"Canada's a nice country," Barbara reflected.

"You've been there?" Amy couldn't keep the surprise out of her voice. It seemed unlikely, somehow, that someone who lived in such a remote town could be so widely traveled.

"Yes, I went to a Health Worker Conference there two years ago. We met with the Canadian Indians. It is a beautiful country."

"Dinner's ready," Elizabeth announced from the kitchen, and Amy breathed a secret sigh of relief. She wasn't very good at making conversation with people she didn't know. Besides, she was hungry.

They moved over to the small table, which was a bit rickety and wobbled a little as Elizabeth put the plates down one by one.

Everyone must have been hungry, because it seemed no time at all before dirty dishes were being cleared away. Amy felt wonderfully full.

"I'll put the kettle on," said Elizabeth, as everyone left the table and made themselves comfortable once again.

"Is that cheeky niece of yours coming home for the holidays?" Caroline asked Barbara.

"*Yuwa*," replied Barbara, using the Luritja word for "yes." "She's coming in tomorrow with Jack."

"Are you talking about Lana?" asked Elizabeth.

"*Yuwa*," said Barbara again. "She's going to boarding school in Alice Springs now."

"Lana must be about your age, Amy," said Caroline. "It'll be nice for you to have some company. Not just adults."

. Amy nodded. That was true. "I hope she speaks English," she thought secretly.

It had been a big day, full of new experiences. Amy felt that she'd been plucked from everything she'd ever known and thrown onto another planet. It was all a bit overwhelming, like living in a dream.

Now with a full stomach and a comfortable chair, she felt her eyelids heavy with fatigue. She could hear the voices of the women talking, but they seemed, all of a sudden, to be far away.

"What do you think, Amy?" she heard vaguely, and again, ". . . Amy?" Then soft laughter. "I knew she was tired, but I didn't realize she was that exhausted."

"Poor girl . . ." And then the voices faded completely from her consciousness as Amy fell into a very deep sleep.

4
Lana

Amy slept late the next morning and when she awoke at last, she found that she had the house all to herself. There was a message scribbled on a scrap of paper lying on the table. Caroline had gone over to the health clinic and would be back at midday. Amy checked her watch and was surprised to see that it was almost that time already!

She made herself some toast and was halfway through the second slice when she heard a car pull up outside.

"Ah, you're up," said her aunt as she came in the door with her arms full of papers. "And I see you managed to find yourself some breakfast—or should I say lunch. Sorry about leaving you alone like that, but I didn't want to disturb you. You were so sound asleep and I just had to pick up a few things at the clinic."

"It's OK," Amy smiled. "And it was no problem finding where everything was. You keep things exactly the way you used to in your Melbourne house."

Caroline laughed and heaped the pile of papers on the other end of the table.

"Do you feel like a swim later today?" she asked.

Amy nodded enthusiastically. "Is there a pool here?"

"No," replied her aunt. "Well, not a pool like the ones in Melbourne. This is a rock pool up in the hills just out of town. We have to drive a short way to get there."

"I thought this was a desert," said Amy.

"It is," Caroline answered. "But there are still a few water holes scattered here and there."

Amy could think of nothing better than a cool swim. The house was very hot and the air so dry. A moment later she realized that she hadn't packed her swimsuit. "I didn't think we'd go swimming," she explained to her aunt in a mournful voice.

"Don't worry about it," Caroline replied, in her usual down-to-earth manner. "No one here has swimsuits."

"You don't mean I have to go naked!" Amy was aghast. "No way! Not in a million years."

"No," Caroline laughed. "Just wear your panties. That's what everyone else does."

Amy digested this information in silence.

"Nothing," she promised herself, "nothing will induce me to go into the water in my underwear." But as the day wore on and the heat increased in its ferocity, the thought of dipping into a cool water hole became more and more attractive. By mid-afternoon her modesty had been forgotten almost completely.

She was actually relieved when she heard a car pull up outside at last. It tooted twice and Caroline pulled back the curtain, which had been drawn against the heat of the day.

"It's Barbara," she announced. "Let's go!"

Soon they were traveling down a beaten old track that led off the main road and sidled up toward the range of mountains perched on the outskirts of town.

Barbara drove with Caroline seated beside her on the front seat. Amy sat in the back of the car, which was overflowing with Aboriginal children of all ages and sizes talking excitedly in their own language. Amy noticed that several of the children had blond hair that stuck out at all angles like dry straw.

Squashed in beside Amy was Barbara's niece.

"Lana. They said she was cheeky," thought Amy. "Rude's a better description!" She couldn't see anything cheeky about this sullen girl. The only thing

Lana had said since her reluctant introduction was a short hello before turning away and saying something under her breath to a friend.

Amy felt hurt and lonely. She was different from all these other children and felt left out of all the fun and excitement. Blinking back her tears, she turned to look out the window. The country was changing and Amy saw that they were slowly climbing up a gradual slope. The red ground was becoming stony, and soon boulders began to dot the landscape here and there. Barbara slowed down as the road surface became quite rough and the children were thrown around a little by the jolts and bumps.

"I'll put her into four-wheel drive now," Barbara said, stopping the car and shifting gears.

There were so many questions about the land that sprang to Amy's mind. She wished that she could ask Lana, but it was obvious that she had no friend there. The girl sat with her back toward Amy, her black curls blowing in the breeze. Amy noticed a braided bracelet on Lana's right wrist. Ribbons in the red, black, and yellow of the Aboriginal flag snaked around each other in an intricate design. Amy remembered having seen the flag on the television news.

This time, it really did turn out to be a short trip, as Caroline had promised a disbelieving Amy. After half an hour they stopped and the children spilled out the back doors shouting with excitement. Lana, who was older than the others, got up more sedately and stepped down, completely ignoring Amy.

Amy sat there sadly, wishing she'd never come.

"Come on, young lady." Caroline's face peered into the back. "You'll get left behind if you don't hurry."

"Good!" thought Amy, but moved over and clambered down on to the stony ground.

"So, Amy. What do you think of this little oasis?" asked Caroline, sweeping her arm across the landscape.

Amy drew her breath in wonder. It was beautiful, and some of her sadness dropped away as she took in the scenery with wide eyes.

They were standing on a little rocky beach and in front of her a sheer rock face rose majestically to meet the sky. A water hole had been eroded out of the red rock at the foot of the cliff and lay shadowed from the late afternoon sun. The water looked so inviting— cool and still, a mirror of dark green.

The peace was soon shattered as a dozen small children splashed in, shrieking with joy. Amy watched as they dived in and came up laughing, pushing wet hair out of their eyes. She noticed that most wore their underpants, although a few of the very little children were naked.

"Come on," said a voice at her shoulder. It was Caroline, and Amy's jaw dropped as she watched her aunt walk gingerly over the rocks to the water's edge clad only in her underwear.

"Oh, it's beautiful," Caroline sighed, as she sank into the coolness and made ripples with her arms.

Amy saw that Barbara and Lana were also now in the water, making their way with slow easy strokes to the far side of the pool. She was the only person left standing on dry land—a monument to modesty.

"Oh, well," she thought, feeling quite reckless. "Here goes." She pulled her dress up over her head and put it on a rock, thinking, "Thank goodness I brought panties with good elastic."

The water was as lovely as it had promised to be. It enveloped Amy in a cool embrace and took away all the dusty, hot, sweaty irritation.

"I don't care if they all hate me," she said to herself as she splashed water into her face.

Caroline was playing a game of chase with some of the little children, pretending that she was a crocodile. The children shrieked in delighted terror as she approached them with arms snapping, and then dived out of her reach.

"She really seems to fit in here," thought Amy. It seemed to emphasize how out of place she felt.

The afternoon shadows were lengthening when Amy eventually clambered out of the water hole. She wrapped herself in a towel and sat on a large rock at one end of the beach next to a clump of bulrushes. Carefully she wrung the water out of her long braid before tossing it back over her shoulder.

The noise of footsteps on the stony ground behind her made her start and turn. It was Lana. The girl scowled as she flounced herself down on another rock. "Barbara says I've got to talk to you," she announced in a cold voice.

Amy was taken aback and sat trying to think of a suitable reply.

"Haven't you white girls got tongues? Can't you talk?" the girl jeered.

"Yes, I have actually," replied Amy, and stuck it out as rudely as possible in Lana's direction and then wished she hadn't been quite so childish. "I'm quite OK on my own thank you very much," she added. She didn't need anyone's company, especially this dreadful girl's.

"*On your own*, eh?" The girl mimicked Amy, a look of disdain all over her face. "Listen. You wouldn't last even one minute in this country *on your own*."

"Yeah, well I just got here, didn't I," retorted Amy. She lowered her voice. "I'd like to see you in

Melbourne. You wouldn't even be able to find Flinders Street station, I'll bet!"

"Who'd want to," Lana snorted in reply, and looked away.

"Well who'd want to live in this awful place. It must be the worst place in the world. That's what my dad thinks anyway. Nothing but sand and spinifex." Amy felt a sob well up in her throat. "And very unfriendly people."

"You think Aboriginal people are unfriendly?" Lana kept on relentlessly. "We didn't kill thousands of you whitefellas. No, it was the other way around. Your ancestors thought they'd get rid of all the blackfellas. Now that's what I call unfriendly."

"That's lies," Amy said under her breath.

"It's not a lie. It's the truth."

"They never taught us that in history at school . . ." Amy's voice trailed off as the sobs reached the surface and she burst into tears.

"Hey, stop that, stop that," Lana whispered desperately, looking around. "If Auntie Barb hears you, I'll be in for it."

Amy held her towel up to her eyes.

"Sorry," Lana said, a hint of genuine regret in her voice. "I didn't mean to make you cry."

"Well, I don't usually," sniffed Amy. "Actually I'm

quite tough, but well, this is all so new . . ." They sat for a while in silence, both feeling a little ashamed.

"Here's a cold drink." Caroline had been back to the car and now approached the girls with a cup in each hand.

"Everything OK?" she asked.

"Yes, fine," replied Amy, hoping that her eyes weren't too red. "It's really lovely here."

Caroline smiled and wandered off to help a small child who was struggling to get his T-shirt over his head.

"What are you doing here, anyway?" Lana asked when they were alone again.

"I'm just here for a couple of weeks," Amy sighed, "while Dad's at an important conference in Canada. Couldn't take me, so I got shoved out here."

"What about your mom? Couldn't she look after you?" Lana asked.

"Haven't got one," Amy answered.

Lana was silent. Then she said softly, "Me neither."

"What? You haven't got a mom either?" Amy tried not to sound too surprised.

"No." The girl turned her head and looked away. The sky was darkening as the evening crept upon them and the horizon blushed pale pink. The rock face beyond the water hole had become a black wall of shadow.

"Have you ever climbed to the top of this mountain?" Amy asked.

"No," replied Lana. "No one goes up there."

"Why not?"

"Not allowed." Amy saw her shift uncomfortably. "There's things up there. I don't know what you'd call them in your language."

"Like ghosts?" Amy asked in a hushed voice.

"I suppose . . . something like that."

A shudder ran down Amy's back and she was relieved when the voice of her aunt broke the spell. It was time for everyone to get back into the car.

The homeward trip was quiet, as tired, happy children huddled together. The heat of the day had left with the sun and it had become quite cool.

Everyone was delivered safely home.

"See you later," Amy said to Lana as she got down from the car.

It was quite dark, but Amy thought she saw a smile as the girl replied, "Yeah, see you."

Amy lay awake in her narrow camp bed that night, staring into the darkness and listening to Caroline's gentle breathing in the bed beside her.

She heard her aunt sigh.

"You awake?" Amy asked softly.

"Hmm?" Caroline rolled over. "What is it?"

"Is it true that lots of Aboriginal people were killed when white people first came to Australia?" Amy spoke into the darkness.

Caroline was silent, then she answered in a hushed voice, "Yes . . . yes, it is, unfortunately, and some killings were not all that long ago. Some of the old people who live here lost family in those massacres. That sort of thing happened in most parts of Australia. Sometimes settlers used rifles; others poisoned the water holes or put strychnine in the flour.

"Mind you, Amy, I don't want to give you the wrong idea. Not all settlers were like that. Many tried hard to learn to live side by side with the Aborigines. It wasn't all bad."

"But why don't they teach us this at school?" asked Amy. "Don't they think it's important?"

"They're too ashamed," Caroline replied. "It's been one of this country's best-kept secrets until relatively recently."

"I didn't think Australia was like this." Amy felt cross and hurt. So much for her great country.

"Oh," her aunt said and sighed deeply. "People are the same all over the world, really. We might look different, have different colored skins, dress in different clothes and worship different gods. But, basically we are all the same, with our fears, ignorance, and prejudice. Hopefully one day as the people of the world learn more about each other, we'll all get along better."

There was silence, then Caroline asked, "Has Lana been talking to you about massacres?"

"Yes."

"I hope she hasn't been deliberately upsetting you. I know that her Uncle Jack fills her head with a lot of anger against white people sometimes," said Caroline. "Aboriginal people can be racist, too, you know."

Amy thought for a moment. "You mean, Lana's Uncle Jack doesn't like white people because our ancestors killed his ancestors."

"Well, yes, but it's a little more complicated than that. There are a lot of people in Australia who are very racist and give Aboriginal people a very hard time. Jack has had a difficult life. He was taken away from his mother when he was only five because his father was a white man. She was a loving mother and people have told me that it broke her heart when they took Jack away from her. She still lives here and you may meet her. Jack's father was a white cattle rancher and no one knows where he is now. Anyway, they put Jack in a foster home where he was very unhappy. They were very cruel days."

"Did Jack tell you all this?" Amy asked.

"No," replied Caroline. "Barbara told me. She is his half sister—same mother but different father. There was a time that she was very worried about him. He'd been into Alice Springs to try to get work but no one would hire him. That may have been racism, too. A lot of people assume that just because a person is Aboriginal, they'll go off on walkabout—not turn up to work. But Jack's not like that. I've seen him work here in this town and he's a good worker and very reliable."

"It doesn't sound very fair," said Amy, taking in every word.

"No, it's not." Caroline rolled over and Amy saw a flash of luminescence from her aunt's watch.

"Look, Amy. It's midnight. We'd better stop talking and get to sleep. I've got to work tomorrow. We can talk more about this in the morning if you want to."

"OK," Amy sighed and then yawned. She was very tired but she lay awake for a long time, staring into the dark. She'd had so many new experiences over the last couple of days. How different it all was!

After a while, she found her thoughts drifting back to Melbourne, her home and her father. It would be dark and cold down on the beach. Maybe there was a wind blowing, driving waves up to the foot of their favorite beach house. The boats moored on the water would be tossed about in the sea.

Her thoughts turned back to the conversation with her aunt, and she began wondering about those first tall ships that had sailed to Australia two hundred years ago. At school she'd learned about how convicts had been brought here to Australia against their will, how much they had suffered, and how, despite all the hardship, they had forged this great land out of nothing. She'd been told that the Aborigines were peace-loving and had given up all their land willingly without much of a fight.

But now, for the first time, she realized that there had been a darker side—those who came with guns and hate in their hearts; those who set out to conquer and dominate by whatever means it took; those prepared to kill.

No wonder there was resentment still among some Aboriginal people. Amy didn't know what to feel. It was all so new and confusing. And how could she explain to Lana that it wasn't her fault?

Amy sighed and turned over. She'd think more about it tomorrow.

5
Grandmother

The next morning, Amy and Caroline walked the short distance to the health clinic.

"I'll just get ready for the radio 'sched,' " said Caroline, consulting her watch. "You can come and take a look."

Amy had no idea what her aunt was talking about, but she followed her into one of the small rooms in the clinic building. A long bench at one end of the room was covered with radio equipment. They sat down and Caroline grabbed a pen and a pad of paper.

"This is how we check on our patients who are in Alice Springs Hospital," she explained.

She turned a few dials on the two-way radio and picked up the microphone, which was attached by a long black spiral cord. A flick of a switch and the radio crackled to life.

Through the static a woman's voice could be heard, but Amy found it difficult to understand a word that was being said. It sounded as though the woman was speaking through a hollow pipe from the bottom of the ocean. And to make matters worse, the sound kept fading away to nothing every now and again.

"Is it English?" asked Amy.

"Yes," replied her aunt. "You wouldn't believe it, would you! The reception is very bad today. Sometimes it works better if we turn the air-conditioning off. Goodness knows why. It sounds as though we'll have to turn it off today. Just a minute." Caroline disappeared for a moment, leaving Amy staring at the array of switches, dials, and buttons. She wondered what would happen if she pushed a few.

Caroline soon returned. "That's a little better—I think," she said unconvincingly as the radio continued its crackling and whining.

"Victor Mike Six Romeo Yankee. Victor Mike Six Romeo Yankee. Do you read me? Over," the voice on the radio crackled.

Amy watched as Caroline sprang into action. "That's our 'call sign,'" she said. She grabbed the microphone and held it up close to her mouth.

"This is Victor Mike Six Romeo Yankee . . . Receiving . . . Over."

"Roger. I've got eight patients to report. Repeat, eight patients. Over," the voice continued.

"That's eight patients. Over," Caroline confirmed.

"Roger. The first is Sheila Nakamarra, eighteen months old. Diagnosed as having pneumonia. Is doing well and will be ready for discharge in . . ." The voice faded and the last part of the message was lost.

"I'm sorry, VJD," Caroline spoke slowly and clearly. "We lost the last bit of the report. Say again. Over."

"Roger," the voice crackled again.

The schedule continued, with Amy straining to understand the messages. Caroline seemed to have little trouble and sat busily writing down all the details.

At last it was finished. "Thanks, VJD. Over and out." Caroline replaced the microphone on the bench and flicked a switch, turning the radio off.

"Well, now I have all the information we need for the patients' relatives. I must tell Elizabeth that Susie had a little girl last night."

"I don't know how you understand a word that comes out of that contraption," said Amy, shaking her head.

"It comes with practice," Caroline smiled. "Come here. I'll show you how we call the Flying Doctor in emergencies. Don't look worried. I don't expect you'll ever have to do it, but it doesn't hurt to know these things."

Caroline showed Amy how to set the correct frequency and turn the radio on.

"See this red button?" she said. "This is the one you push to get the attention of the radio station in Alice Springs. That's VJD, RFDS—the Royal Flying Doctor Service. If you hold this button down firmly for fifteen seconds, it rings some sort of alarm in the Alice radio station. Then they call you back to find out what you want. After that, you just speak into the microphone, keeping it close to your mouth. You have to push this little button on the side of the microphone to make it work."

Amy watched with interest.

Caroline placed the microphone back on the bench and turned to her niece. "Now, what am I going to do with you? You'll be bored stiff after half an hour of watching me work." She looked thoughtful. "I did explain to your father that I wouldn't be able to get time off work and that this would probably not be a very suitable place for you to stay, but . . ." She broke off when she saw the uncomfortable look on Amy's face. She said more gently, "But it is really lovely to see you again."

"I don't mind watching you . . ." Amy started to say.

"There you are," a voice from behind her exclaimed. "I've been looking for you everywhere!"

It was Lana. Amy felt surprised and strangely pleased. After the events of the previous day, she'd been uncertain if she'd see Lana again. After all, they hadn't exactly hit it off.

"Ah, there you go," said Caroline, relieved. "Lana can keep you occupied. Actually . . ." she paused and delved into one of her uniform's deep pockets. "Take this money and buy yourself a good hat at the store. Oh, and some sunblock, too. Some of the strong stuff. The sun is pretty vicious out here and I can't send you back to your father looking like a lobster."

The two girls wandered out through the clinic building. Amy saw Barbara dressed in a blue uniform, busy applying a length of white bandage to a small child's leg.

"Is your auntie a nurse?" asked Amy.

"*Wiya*, no," replied Lana. "She's an Aboriginal Health Worker. It's the same sort of thing as a nurse really, I guess, except that they understand the Aboriginal ways firsthand."

Amy felt the sun pound down on her bare head as they stepped outside. All around them the red sand, blue sky, and white-walled houses seemed to reflect the heat and light, magnifying it many times over. It was very hot and Amy felt the beads of sweat forming already on her brow. Yes, it would be a good idea to buy a hat.

"Where's the store?" she asked Lana.

"Just down the road a little way," the girl replied, gesturing with one arm.

"Just down the road! That can mean anything around here," she thought, remembering the long drive from Alice Springs.

They wandered on down the road, scuffing the red sand with their feet. Soon they were passing what had once been a house. It was only a skeleton now, with a few crooked uprights and an occasional floorboard.

"What happened here?" asked Amy.

"Oh, the people pulled it down," Lana said, and then saw the look of amazement on Amy's face.

"It was a stupid house, anyway," she continued. "You couldn't live in it. The walls were in all the wrong places and it was stinking hot because the breeze couldn't blow through. Some government builder guy thought he knew best, but he should have asked us first. Then we might have gotten a house that was useful."

"I see," replied Amy, "but why did they pull it down?"

"Someone died here," said Lana, and seeing Amy still looking puzzled, went on. "When someone dies in a house like this, everyone has to leave. The person's spirit stays until the proper ceremonies are carried out. That's what happened here. My grandfather died and everyone moved out. In fact, no one ever wanted to live there again."

Amy digested this information in silence. Things were certainly done differently around here. She kicked at a stone on the road, sending red dust flying. Her once-white sneakers had become a brownish, orange color.

"Where do you live?" she asked.

"Usually with Auntie Irene in Alice Springs," Lana replied. "My Uncle Jack is pretty tough on me. He says I've got to get some education. But I hate school."

"What about when you're here. Where do you stay?"

"Oh, here and there," Lana answered with a shrug of her shoulders. "Mostly with Auntie Barbara."

Amy thought back to her comfortable little house tucked in the suburbs of Melbourne. Just her and Dad. Oh, and Emma sometimes. Emma, Emma—she quickly pushed the thought of her dad's girlfriend to the back of her mind again.

"It must be nice to have lots of family," she said with a sigh.

But Lana didn't reply and when Amy turned, she saw that her friend was busy waving to someone.

"That's my grandmother," explained Lana. "Over there at her *wiltja*. Come and meet her. They call her Old Ruby around here."

Lana led Amy off the road and toward a curved iron shelter such as Amy had seen on her arrival in the town. The sand became thick and soft beneath their feet.

They passed an old man who was hunched over a canvas, a stick in one hand. He looked up briefly before returning to his work. Dipping his stick into some yellow paint, he carefully applied another dot of color to his painting. Amy would have liked to stop and watch, but Lana signaled to her to follow her over to the curved iron *wiltja*.

Here an old lady sat on a faded blanket at one end of the shelter, a large dog stretched out asleep behind her. A fire smoked a little to one side.

As the girls approached, Amy recognized the old lady. She was the woman who'd sat opposite her in the car on the journey from Alice Springs. She remembered the red scarf and the large, brown growth on her lip.

The old woman looked up with unseeing eyes. "Nangala?" she asked in a toothless, croaky voice. "Nangala?"

Lana replied in Luritja. Ruby reached up and pulled her granddaughter down beside her on to the blanket.

"So we've got a visitor," she croaked. "Come closer girl. What's your name?"

Amy couldn't help feeling a little scared. This blind, toothless, ragged old woman was the very image of the witch in all the fairy tales she'd ever known. She trembled a little as she sat down, hoping that the old crone would not grab her arm, too.

But Ruby was busy. "Tea, tea," she mumbled. "Where's my tea kettle?"

Lana got up and fetched a blackened metal kettle from beside the fire. The noise disturbed the dog. It stood up and stretched before ambling away with a disgruntled look on its face.

Lana's grandmother was still muttering, half in English and half in her own tongue, as she grabbed a large cloth bag and felt around inside it. "Might be cups in here . . . *Yuwa!*" She produced three battered enamel mugs and filled each with thick black fluid from the kettle.

"Thank you," said Amy politely, taking the mug from the gnarled old hands.

She sipped at it. The black tea hit her taste buds with what felt like a small explosion. It took all her willpower not to spit the liquid straight back out. This was the strongest, sweetest tea she had ever tasted in her life. She looked sideways at Lana who was sipping hers without any apparent problem, and then carefully put the mug down on the ground beside the blanket.

Amy blinked and wished fervently that she had a large, cold glass of water to wash away the taste that lingered in her mouth.

Her thoughts, however, disappeared as she felt a claw hand placed gently on her forearm. She started, looking down at the hand and then up into the old woman's face. The lump on the wrinkled lower lip was wet with spittle.

"You been here before?" Old Ruby asked.

Amy started to shake her head, then suddenly remembered that the woman was blind. "No," she said aloud, her voice shaking.

"This is my country, you know," the woman continued. "Look out there." She gestured with one bony arm. Amy turned obediently and gazed out into the redness.

"Yes," she said. "It's very nice, Mrs. . . . Mrs. . . . ." She was lost for words. Lana snickered behind her hand.

"Quiet, Nangala," the old voice wavered. "This girl's got a lot to learn. I'll teach her like I've taught you. Listen to me," she said to Amy. "You come back and I will tell you about this country and its secrets.

I'll tell you the stories of the Dreamtime. You should know them. It's important."

Amy watched the woman's face as she spoke. The white-glazed eyes had widened and almost sparkled with enthusiasm.

"Look," she pointed, grabbing Amy's arm a little harder now. Amy saw that she was pointing toward the mountain range they'd visited the day before.

"That's Women's Dreaming," she said and then swept her arm toward the red plains and spinifex. "That's Kangaroo . . . Malu Dreaming."

Amy didn't really understand what Ruby meant but found herself caught up and carried away by her talk. She listened as the woman spoke and began to feel a little of the wonder and reverence, the worship of the country that was expressed in her voice. It invoked in her the same feelings she'd experienced when her dad had taken her into the big cathedral in Melbourne. That day the church organ had been playing such beautiful music, it had stirred something deep within her.

The spell was broken when Lana spoke, saying something quietly in Luritja. The old woman looked disappointed.

Lana turned to Amy. "I just told her that we had better go. We have to get to the store and buy you a hat before it closes. And before you get too sun-burned!"

Old Ruby held Amy's hand tightly. "You come back and see me, girl," she croaked. "You must learn. All right? *Palya?*"

"I will," said Amy and meant it. Just then she noticed the mug of tea beside her on the ground, still full, and felt guilty. She didn't want to offend this woman who'd offered her such kindness.

"She won't notice," thought Amy as she quietly tipped the last of the tea into the sand and handed the empty mug back to the woman.

"Thank you very much for the tea," she said with her best Melbourne manners. But as she turned to leave, she heard the woman chuckle and knew she'd fooled no one.

"Why doesn't she have that lump removed," Amy asked her friend, once they were out of earshot.

"What lump?" asked Lana.

"Ha, ha, very funny. The one on her lip, of course."

Lana stopped dead in her tracks, and Amy watched as her friend's face changed from surprise to amuse-ment. And then Lana held her stomach and laughed and laughed.

"That's not a lump," she gasped between her merry gales.

"What is it, then?" asked Amy, feeling very put out by this extraordinary behavior. "A pink elephant?"

"No!" Lana stopped laughing and cleared her throat. "It's chewing tobacco. You know, the same stuff that's in cigarettes. A lot of women here chew it instead of smoking. It's just as bad for you. When they're not chewing, they rest the tobacco on their lip."

"Really? Is that true?" asked Amy, a little skeptical. Lana nodded.

They walked on in silence, Amy thinking about the old woman and Lana laughing a little to herself.

"She called you Nangala," Amy said at last. "Does that mean granddaughter?"

"No," Lana replied. "That's my Aboriginal name. My skin name."

"Oh," said Amy. "So people have two names?"

"Two at least," Lana replied with a short laugh. "The Aboriginal one stays the same, but we're not too fussy about the whitefella ones. People change those quite a lot."

"That must be a bit confusing," said Amy.

"Not for us, it isn't," said Lana. "We've got it all worked out. Look." She grabbed a stick and crouched down in the sand. First she smoothed a piece of ground, then scratched some letters in the sand.

N A N G A L A. "Nangala," she said.

"Now," Lana continued, as Amy knelt down beside her, "there are eight different skin names—that is, eight for men and eight for women—and what you're called determines where you belong in the community. That is, it tells you who you call auntie or sister, who you can marry, who you're not allowed to talk to—that sort of thing."

She wrote more names in the sand: NAPANGARTI and TJAMPITJINPA. "Now, those are my mother and father's skin names. My sisters are all 'Nangala' like me, and all my brothers are 'Tjangala.' You see, they start with a 'TJ' instead of an 'N.' Do you see?"

"I think so," said Amy uncertainly.

Lana took a deep breath, and went on. "Now, when I marry, I have to marry a 'Tjungurrayi' and my children will all be 'Napaltjarri' for a girl, or 'Tjapaltjarri' for a boy. See? Simple!"

"I'm glad you think so," said Amy, looking with a puzzled expression at the confused mass of strange names etched in the ground.

"You know that you've got a skin name, don't you?" said Lana, as they started walking again.

"Have I?" exclaimed Amy, delighted. Maybe she could fit in here after all.

"*Yuwa*," nodded Lana. "Usually you don't get a skin name until you've been here for a while and look like staying. But you see, your Auntie Caroline has one. She's called 'Nampitjinpa.'"

"Well?" asked Amy. "So what's my name?"

"You're 'Nangala' too," smiled Lana. "You're my skin sister."

6
Tricky Ricky

"Here, try this one." Lana giggled as she put a white terry-cloth hat on Amy's head.

"No way!" Amy protested. "I wouldn't be seen dead in this."

"Well, how about this one then?" Lana produced a blue cap with Mickey Mouse grinning above the brim.

"No thanks. This is more my style." Amy picked up a black felt cowboy hat with red ribbon trim.

"They'll think you want a job as a rancher," teased Lana.

But Amy didn't answer. She was busy admiring herself in an old cracked mirror that was propped up next to the pile of hats. Yes, this was the hat for her!

"And how can I help you young ladies?" an unpleasant voice drawled from behind them. The girls turned with a start.

"Oh, it's you Miss Lana," the man continued. "I should have known. Now listen, just choose a hat and get out. OK?"

Amy watched as the man slunk off to serve another customer at the checkout. He walked like a goanna—a big lizard—his short stubby legs turned out at the knees.

"That's Rick," whispered Lana. "I should have warned you about him. He's the store manager and a real pig."

Amy had to agree. She'd taken an instant dislike to the man. It had been something about his pale blue eyes. They were the sort of eyes that always seemed to be looking over your shoulder and not at you squarely and honestly. The look of slightly vacant innocence sat out of place in his sour, pasty white face, and a lifetime of sneering had left its mark in deep lines around his mouth and on his forehead. No, he wasn't to be trusted.

"Come on." Amy tugged at Lana's shirtsleeve. "Let's find the sunblock and get out of here."

"Wait a minute. I'll just get a cold drink." Lana strolled over to a large refrigerator, deliberately taking her time and opened one of the heavy glass doors. She stood scratching her head as she surveyed the drinks and eventually selected two containers of orange juice.

"Do you want one?" she asked Amy.

"Yes, please." Amy nodded. "Now, where's the sunblock?"

"Just over here."

"Come on. Hurry up," yelled Rick. "It's closing time. And would you mind not standing there with the fridge door open?"

Lana closed the refrigerator door with unnecessary force and turned back toward the shelves of groceries.

"Here's the sunblock." She grabbed a bottle off a shelf and handed it to Amy.

"Come on," Rick yelled again.

"OK, OK!" Lana answered crossly.

"Don't you give me that attitude, girl. You're far too cheeky for your own good. You'll get yourself into trouble one day if you don't watch that tongue of yours." Rick sneered unpleasantly. He checked the prices on the hat, sunblock, and drinks, banging each down on the counter in turn.

"Right," he said when he'd finished. "That's thirty-eight dollars." He put out his hand.

"Thirty-eight dollars?" protested Lana. "That seems an awful lot."

"Just pay it!" he ordered. "And then get out."

"Come on, Lana." Amy spoke softly at her shoulder. "Don't upset him. Let's just go." She felt quite frightened by this aggressive man. She gave him some notes which he snatched from her hand. The cash register rang and he slammed the change down on the counter.

"Right, now get out of here!" he said and turned away.

The girls didn't wait to be told again. They hurried out on to the road and began to walk back toward the clinic building. Amy put on her new hat.

"Very nice," said Lana approvingly. "I'm just sorry we had to buy it from Tricky Ricky's store. The trouble is, it's the only store we have here."

"He's very rude. Of course, you did upset him on purpose," said Amy.

"I just can't help it. He annoys me so much. As well as being a horrible person, he's a lousy store manager. He only opens the shop for a few hours a day and he overcharges. Food here costs about four times as much as in Alice Springs." Lana kicked at the sand in annoyance.

"Why don't the people here get rid of him?" asked Amy.

"Good question," replied Lana. "I really don't know. Maybe he knows someone important on the town council or something. One thing I know for sure though—he's up to no good."

Amy had been about to ask what she meant by "up

to no good" when her thoughts were interrupted by the sound of an engine coughing to life somewhere back down the road. A moment later they had to shield their eyes from a cloud of dust flung up by a car that hurtled past, traveling far too fast.

"You idiot!" shouted Lana, shaking her fist after the disappearing vehicle.

"Who was that?" exclaimed Amy.

"Who else—Ricky!" replied Lana. "He's in a big hurry."

"Where's he going?" asked Amy.

Lana shook her head. "I don't know," she said and fell into a thoughtful silence.

Amy saw the clinic building in the distance as they turned the corner. She wondered what her aunt thought about the town's strange shop manager.

A few minutes later, she heard another car coming up the road behind them. This one traveled at a much more sedate pace. She turned and saw a blue Holden approaching. It slowed as it approached.

"Two cars in five minutes," said Lana with a smile. "This is rush hour, outback style. Hey, it's Uncle Jack."

The car pulled up beside them and a man stuck his head out the window.

"Lana! Get in the car now," he ordered in a rough voice.

"I'll just walk Amy back to the . . ." Lana started.

"Don't argue," Jack interrupted. "Just get in. I'm taking you home."

Jack looked toward Amy, who felt herself shrink under the hard gaze. Never before in her life had she been looked at with such blatant dislike. She wished she could hide and had a sudden urge to run to the clinic and the protection of her aunt.

Lana stood her ground for a moment, scuffing her feet, but then obviously thought better of causing a scene. She walked slowly toward her uncle, head hanging. Just as she was about to get into the car, she managed to shoot a look at Amy that said, "Don't worry. We'll see each other again soon."

The door slammed and Jack revved the engine.

As the car disappeared down the road, Amy sighed. She walked on, a lonely little figure in a black cowboy hat surrounded by a haze of red dust.

7
Emergency!

Bang! Bang! Bang! Amy sat bolt upright in bed, the skin pricking on the back of her neck.

The next minute a light snapped on and she saw Caroline sitting on the edge of the bed rubbing her eyes.

Bang! Bang! Someone was hammering at the front door.

"Two o'clock in the morning," groaned Caroline. "It must be an emergency." She stood up and threw a bathrobe over her nightgown.

"Stay there, Amy," she said in a voice thick with sleep. "I'll just find out what's going on."

Amy lay down again, closed her eyes, and strained to hear the conversation at the front door. She couldn't make out exact words but caught the tone of urgency in the voices.

"It's an emergency all right," said Caroline as she appeared back in the bedroom. "It's Old Ruby. She's having another of her bad spells."

Amy sat up again. "Can I come with you?"

Caroline pulled her uniform over her head. "I don't think you'd better this time, Amy. It might not be very . . . well . . . suitable."

"Please, Caroline," pleaded Amy in her most mournful voice. "I promise I won't get in the way. Besides, I don't want to stay here all alone."

Caroline stood for a moment, hands on hips, looking at her niece. Then she gave a quick nod. "OK." She turned to get her bag and Amy heard her mutter under her breath: "I don't know what her father would think of this."

Amy dressed quickly before her aunt had a chance to change her mind, and soon they were out the door and into the dark of night.

A car was waiting for them, the engine idling quietly and the headlights glaring. Barbara was at the wheel and she leaned over to open the door at the passenger side. "We'd better hurry," she said anxiously. "I haven't seen Ruby this bad before."

"Have you got the emergency box and oxygen?" Caroline asked as she and Amy climbed into the front seat.

"Yes, I stopped off at the clinic first," Barbara replied. She put the car into gear and pulled out on to the road.

The town looked very different at night. Amy felt quite disorientated, which was partly due to not being fully awake. She rubbed her eyes and looked blearily out the window. A few sparse streetlights cast dim shadows, but as they moved to the edge of town, there was no light at all. The car's bright headlights lit a strip of road before them.

"Here we are," announced Barbara a few minutes later. "I'll turn the car so that we get some light from the headlights on to Ruby."

"Quick, *quick!*" A young woman met Barbara at the car window and spoke anxiously in Luritja.

"You'd better stay in the car, Amy," ordered Caroline.

Amy would normally have complained about being left out, but this time she held her tongue. She had heard the serious tone in her aunt's voice and besides, she wasn't sure if she could face seeing Old Ruby sick. She might faint or something and then there would be two patients instead of one!

In the headlight beam she could see a group of people standing near the curved iron *wiltja*, the crumpled figure of the old woman at their feet. Caroline was crouched down doing something, but it was too far for Amy to see exactly what was going on.

"Psst," a voice beside her hissed. Amy jumped and turned to the window. It was Lana. "Come on," the girl whispered. "Get out and wait with me here."

"But Caroline said . . . " Amy began and then stopped. It wasn't much fun sitting all by herself in the car. She opened the door and climbed down.

"What's happening?" she whispered back.

"It's my grandmother," said Lana and Amy heard her voice tremble a little. "She's talking funny. It's a bit scary." Amy looked at her friend, but it was hard to make out her features in the darkness of the night.

"Come a bit closer. Let's see if we can hear what's happening," Lana urged.

Amy felt her pulse quicken as they edged toward the circle of people.

"It's all right, Ruby. You're OK," Caroline was saying in a gentle soothing voice. "Barbara, could you ask the people if she had a fit?"

Amy heard Barbara's voice translating the question and saw the shaking heads. No . . . not a fit.

The two girls were close enough now to see the old woman's face quite clearly. It was contorted in fear, the white eyes staring widely and her toothless mouth hanging open. She began to talk, slowly at first and then faster and faster until the words tumbled over one another. A moment later, without warning, she sat bolt upright and the circle of people stepped back with a cry of surprise. The woman grabbed at her hair and pulled the red scarf off, throwing it to one side. Then she folded her body forward as though in pain and began rocking on her heels, moaning softly.

"Barbara?" Caroline asked quietly. "Do you think we should get the *ngangkere*?"

"*Yuwa*," said Barbara. "Yes, I think so." She spoke to a woman beside her, who left hurriedly.

"What's happening?" Amy asked in a small, frightened voice. She had never seen anything like this before in her life.

"They're getting the *ngangkere*. He's the Aboriginal doctor who uses traditional ways of healing," Lana said softly.

Barbara fetched a large red box from the back of the car.

Amy watched as Caroline placed an oxygen mask over Ruby's face. A minute later the rocking stopped and the old woman slumped forward with her head in her hands. Caroline put an arm around the frail old shoulders and cradled the tousled head at her shoulder, speaking soothingly all the while.

"Now she'll be all right." Lana's voice was full of relief. "Every time this happens, I wonder if maybe she might, well . . ." Her voice trailed off.

"Has it happened before?" asked Amy.

"*Yuwa*," said Lana. "This is the third time I've seen it. Mind you, this time her talk was a bit different."

"How?" asked Amy. "What do you mean?" She hadn't understood anything the woman had said.

"Well . . ." Lana stopped. There was a waver of fear in her voice as she continued. "She was saying some . . . odd things."

Amy didn't reply. Lana's fear had blown across her like a cool breeze and she felt goose bumps prickle the skin of her arms. She hugged herself and shivered.

Lana was still talking. "Something about her country and that it must be protected; that the law must be protected. She kept saying: 'Don't let them do it,' over and over. And then she said . . ." Lana stopped again and Amy heard her sigh.

"What Lana?" she asked. "What did she say?"

Lana's voice had dropped to a faint whisper. The words were so soft that Amy found herself straining to hear. "She said that someone was going to die."

A sudden noise caused the two girls to turn in fright. Silhouetted against the headlights, in a haze of dust, stood a man.

"It's Jack," whispered Lana, and as she spoke the man moved forward so that light fell across his face. Amy saw that her friend was right.

But Jack had not noticed the two girls. He stood watching the scene in front of the curved iron shelter—watching the circle of women. Barbara was packing things back into the emergency box and Caroline still cradled the poor old woman's head in her arms. The look on his face was indescribable, a mixture of many emotions that Amy didn't recognize.

"Is she all right?" he demanded gruffly in a loud voice.

Everyone looked around, a little startled.

"She'll be OK," replied Caroline, looking up. "We gave her a little oxygen and the *ngangkere*'s on his way. I'll come back tomorrow to give her another complete check. She'll sleep now."

Jack didn't say anything. He turned to go but stopped as he caught sight of Amy and Lana sitting close together, staring up at him with wide eyes like two frightened possums. He scowled and, turning on his heel, disappeared into the night.

8
Kadaitcha

The two girls had been shaken by the events of the night emergency, and the next day, they were still walking around with long, serious faces. Caroline and Barbara put their heads together and decided that a night out camping by the water hole might help cheer them up.

The following morning, they loaded the car up with baggage, supplies, and a dozen small children and headed out of town.

It was another hot day and everyone welcomed the dip in the cool water beneath the rock wall. Lunch came and went and before they knew it, and shadows began lengthening as the sun relinquished some of its fierce heat.

Amy and Lana swam out to the deepest part of the pool. As they neared the rock wall, Amy saw that it was not as smooth as it appeared from a distance. There were ridges and hollows that would enable you to climb straight up to the top, if you dared. A narrow ridge ran along horizontally just above the water line, and Amy heaved herself up and sat dangling her legs into the water below. Lana soon joined her and leaned back against the rock.

"How is your grandmother now?" Amy asked.

"She seems a little bit better," Lana replied. "But she's sort of sad and isn't eating very much."

"You know how she said that someone was going to die," Amy said after a short pause.

"*Yuwa.*" Lana nodded slowly and looked away.

"Well," Amy continued after taking a big breath, "do you think it's true? Can Old Ruby look into the future? Do you think someone will die?"

Lana didn't answer at once and Amy wondered if she'd heard her question. But then the girl turned and looked Amy squarely in the eyes. "She's never been wrong," she said sadly. "Someone *will* die."

"Who?" Amy's lips formed the word but no sound came out. It didn't matter. Lana saw the question in Amy's eyes and answered with a shrug of her shoulders and a quick shake of her head.

They looked over the water to the little stony beach where happy children were splashing in the shallows. Barbara and Caroline were busy lighting a fire and preparing the camp oven for dinner.

"When did your mom die?" Lana's question took Amy by surprise. She blinked and swallowed.

"The fifth of September—two years ago," she answered in a shaky voice. "It was a car accident." Amy hesitated. Should she go on? Would Lana understand? She took a big breath and continued. "She wasn't killed right away—just unconscious. Dad took me to the hospital to see her. She was in the intensive care ward, tied up to a million machines that breathed for her and had alarms and . . . It was sort of Mom, but it wasn't, too. She died after one week." Amy stopped. She hadn't meant to say so much. In fact it was the first time that she'd been able to tell anyone about her mom since the accident. "That's odd," she thought, in a detached sort of way. That familiar lump was back in her throat, making it difficult to breathe, and her stomach began to hurt like it always did whenever she thought of her mother and how much she missed her. She didn't want to talk about it anymore.

"What about you?" she managed to ask Lana. "What happened to your mom?"

Lana bent her head low so that her chin almost touched her chest. She spoke so softly that Amy had to strain to catch the words.

"She died last year—pneumonia," Lana said. "The nurse—it wasn't Caroline then—she wanted her to go to hospital, but Mom wouldn't go."

Lana stopped and looked at Amy with a strange fierceness in her eyes. "She was proud. There was no way she was going to some whitefella hospital and have some whitefella doctor telling her what was best for her. No way!"

"I see," whispered Amy, not at all sure of the right thing to say.

"It didn't do any good though," said Lana, looking down again and speaking softly once more. "She ended up in an ambulance being raced into Alice Springs unconscious. I was allowed to go in the ambulance with Barbara and the nurse. The ambulance people were really good. They did everything they could, but . . ." Lana dropped her head even further and her words came out in short painful bursts as though she were short of breath. Amy knew that feeling well and put a hand gently on her friend's shoulder.

"She died in . . . in the hospital . . . there in the whitefella hospital that she hated . . . away from her 'country' and everything that's important. I suppose the staff were good, they really tried to help. But there was one nurse that I'll never forget. I heard her talking. They didn't know I could hear. They didn't think I was listening, but I did hear . . ."

Lana was trembling very slightly and Amy slipped her arm around her shoulders. "What did they say?" she asked.

"Well," Lana sniffed and took a breath. "One of the nurses was saying that she didn't know why my mother hadn't come in earlier before she'd gotten so bad—so they could have done something to help, and the other one said . . ." Lana paused and swallowed. "That nurse said, 'Don't worry, it's only some poor Abo from the bush. One less to worry about'!"

"Oh no!" The soft cry left Amy's lips involuntarily and her arm dropped. "Oh, Lana . . ." She saw that Lana's eyes were brimming with tears and was aware that her own eyes were also wet. For a moment they embraced, black curls mingled with wisps of blonde as they shared their pain and loss.

And then they sat quietly, lost in their own thoughts, side by side on the ledge.

"Dinner's ready!" a voice called across the water. The two girls blinked back into the real world.

Amy wiped her eyes and sniffed. "I feel terrible," she said.

"Me too," said Lana, in a nasal voice.

They slid off the ledge and ducked their heads under the cold water.

"Do my eyes look red?" asked Amy when she surfaced. She did not want Caroline to know that she'd been crying.

"They're OK," replied Lana. "What about mine?"

"Fine."

They swam back to the stony beach and joined the other children. Caroline had heated up a huge quantity of spaghetti with tomato sauce and was busy ladling generous helpings onto plastic plates.

It was hard for the two girls to remain glum when they were surrounded by so many smiling children who laughed at each other, sucking up the spaghetti like long worms.

Soon, Amy and Lana were joining in, seeing who could make the loudest, most disgusting slurping sound.

The big meal made Amy feel a little sleepy. She noticed one of the smallest children climb onto Barbara's lap and curl up, rubbing his eyes.

The sun was setting and the glow of the campfire drew everyone in close.

"Do you know how you light a fire with two sticks?" asked Lana, who sat beside her in the semi-dark.

"No, how?" asked Amy. She had heard that Aboriginal people could light a fire this way.

"Make sure one of the sticks is a match." Lana collapsed in laughter, holding her stomach with both hands.

"Very funny," said Amy, rolling her eyes. Then she laughed, too.

A moment later, Barbara called Lana to come and help collect the dirty dishes. Her friend got up, saying something that Amy didn't understand, but guessed might mean, "Why do I always have to do the washing up?" Amy said that to her dad nearly every night back home in Melbourne.

It was strange how she'd found a friend like this out here in the middle of the desert. Lana was different from her friends back in Melbourne. Her city friends had not really understood how she'd felt when she lost her mother, although some tried hard. They'd either ignored her mother's death completely, turning away embarrassed and not knowing what to say, or else they'd gone completely to the other extreme. Amy didn't know which response had been worse: the friends who'd ignored her feelings, or the ones who had insisted on trying to comfort her all the time and treated her like an invalid.

But Lana seemed to understand.

Amy sighed and looked around. Lana was helping Caroline with the washing up. She could see their dark shapes moving down by the water in the last vestiges of sunlight. In the sky, one or two stars had begun to shine and the full round face of the moon hung watching over them.

"Amy." She turned at the sound of Barbara's voice.

"Amy, could you help me unload the baggage from the car?"

The baggage consisted mostly of a dozen or so thin foam mattresses that had been tied onto the car's roof rack. Together, Barbara and Amy pulled them down and dragged them over to the camp. A pile of blankets was collected from the back of the car and little beds made up close to the fire, which glowed redder and redder in the growing dark.

"Here's yours and Lana's," said Barbara. "I saw a nice patch of flat ground just over there." She indicated with a small flashlight.

"Here, I'll help you with that." It was Lana again.

Amy took her mattress and a flashlight, and together the girls made their way over to the other side of the campfire where they found the smooth patch of ground. They put the mattresses side by side and Amy lay down. She could still feel the ground through the thin foam mattress. "Oh well," she thought with a sigh. "It's better than nothing."

"Here, you'll need a blanket." Caroline approached and handed each of them a light cotton blanket. "It can get fairly cold out here at night."

Amy propped herself up on one elbow and watched Caroline and Barbara busily organizing the children into their newly made beds. The happy chatter had subsided and soon silence ensued as one by one they fell into exhausted sleep.

"Have you camped here a lot before, Lana?" Amy asked in a whisper. Silence. "Lana?" Amy turned to look at her friend who was stretched out on the mattress beside her.

"Lana?" she asked again, but again there was no answer. The girl was lying absolutely still, her mouth hanging open. The old woman's words came racing into Amy's mind—"somebody will die"—and for a moment her heart leaped to her mouth. But then Lana gave a deep sigh and rolled over.

Amy relaxed. "She must have been tired," she thought.

The night had become quite cool already, and Amy pulled the thin blanket up around her neck. She could hear her aunt walking around checking that all was well, shining the flashlight beam here and there.

"Good-night, Amy," came a whisper in the dark.

"Good-night, Caroline," she answered, and rolled over onto her back to study the sky.

"I'm sure that there aren't that many stars in the skies above Melbourne," she thought. The darkness above was peppered with pinpoints of white light. "No," she said to herself. "That's silly—it is the same sky after all."

It was very quiet. Amy could hear the occasional sniffle from one of the children and the crackle of the fire, but that was all. Once she imagined she heard what could have been a dingo—a wild dog—howling in the distance, but it was very faint. She thought back to her bedroom in Melbourne, where she could always hear the dull rumble of traffic on the busy highway nearby.

There was a rustle in the bushes over toward the water. Amy once again lifted herself up on one elbow. She was a little worried about sleeping so close to all the creepy-crawlies of the night. The full moon was now very bright and she saw a twisted clump of bush reflecting the silvery light.

"Hmm . . . can't see anything. I hope it wasn't a snake. No, I bet it was one of those cute marsupial mice." Yes, that was a less frightening thought.

She turned to study the water hole. A second moon lay looking up at her, reflected in the black glassy surface of the water. Above it, the rock face loomed, a solid dark mass.

"It's so peaceful," thought Amy and sank back down onto her rough bed. She wriggled a bit to find a spot where her hipbone might mold into the ground beneath a little more comfortably. Then she closed her eyes.

Amy awoke in a cold sweat, the sound of a scream ringing in her ears. Her heart pounded in her chest as she felt Lana grab her arm. They were both sitting bolt upright.

"What's that?" she managed to ask.

A flashlight snapped on and the beam was shone back and forth, searching. A small dark shape emerged from behind the bushes and the flashlight swung back, catching it fully with its light as Amy and Lana stared, wide-eyed.

"Oh, it's only one of the kids," whispered Amy, her voice full of relief, and she heard Lana laugh as the tension melted away.

A small boy scrambled in a panic toward the security of the camp. He stumbled a couple of times and Amy heard him whimpering. He had obviously been frightened very badly.

"Eddie, Eddie!" Barbara picked her way through

the mattresses that were scattered around the fire. Most of the children were now sitting up rubbing their eyes, bewildered by the commotion. She reached the frightened boy in a few quick steps and gathered him firmly into her arms.

"Eddie. What's the matter? Did you see a snake?"

Amy could see the boy shake with fear. He pointed back the way he'd come—over toward the clump of bushes. His mouth opened, but no sound came out.

"Come on, Eddie. You're safe now. Tell me," Barbara coaxed gently. "What did you see?"

"*Ka . . . ka . . . kadaitcha!*" the boy blurted out all at once and then started to cry.

"Are you sure?" Barbara asked, and Amy heard a new note of urgency in her question.

Lana grabbed Amy's arm again, harder this time, and one of the children began to howl.

"What is it?" Amy asked. "What's happening?" She could see Caroline trying desperately to calm a group of children who were all now crying in fear.

"*Kadaitcha*," whispered Lana. "They come when someone needs punishing by tribal law. They use magic. Sometimes they kill."

"We'll have to leave," Amy heard Barbara say. "We can't stay here if there's a *kadaitcha* around. I believe this boy has seen one. We can't take any chances."

"Where did he see it?" Caroline asked.

"It was a light," said Barbara, in a nervous voice. "Up above the rock pool. No one goes there. It's very sacred. No one, that is but . . ." Her voice trailed off mid-sentence.

"What were you going to say?" Caroline asked.

"It must be a *kadaitcha*," she whispered. "I tell you, we can't take any chances. I want to make sure we all get back safely."

"It's all a bit strange," Caroline said thoughtfully. "I'm sure I caught the glimpse of a light up above the water hole as well. The boy wasn't imagining it." She paused, staring up at the solid darkness of the rock wall. "There's a road that leads up to the back of the plateau, isn't there? Maybe someone's lost or needs help."

Barbara shook her head but Caroline continued, "I might just take a quick look. It'd be a shame to have to pack everything up and move everyone for nothing."

"No!" Barbara's voice cut the air. "No, you mustn't go."

"Look, I'm only going a little way up to have a look." Caroline sounded irritated now. "Nothing is going to hurt me."

"You don't understand," said Barbara desperately, and grabbed at Caroline's arm.

But Caroline was too quick and with a defiant shake of her head, she turned on her heel and walked off toward the shadows, flashlight in hand.

"Everyone into the car. Quickly, quickly!" Barbara was panicking. "Leave the mattresses. Leave everything." She said a few more words in Luritja, and soon Amy felt herself caught up in the wave of children and fear that pushed her toward the car.

9
Above the Water Hole

"Caroline!" Barbara yelled again. "Come back!"

Amy turned to see if she could spot her aunt, hoping that she would see her returning to the camp. But Caroline had reached the clump of bush, the light of the flashlight marking her progress. Amy saw her stop and swing the light around in a wide arc.

"Please come back," Amy pleaded quietly to herself. She wanted to leave this suddenly haunted place.

"Oh, no." Lana spoke beside her in the dark. "She's going up the path to the top of the ridge."

"Where?" Amy asked. But the beam from the flashlight answered her question, bobbing a little as her aunt climbed up in the darkness beside the rock face.

"I've got to stop her," Amy said between her teeth. "Look, I'm going after her."

"It's not safe," Lana replied, in a soft insistent voice. "I'm telling you. There are 'things' up there. You won't come back."

But Amy stood watching her aunt climb farther and farther away, disappearing into the darkness. What if she never saw her again? The words of the old woman came back to her and, in an instant, she made up her mind.

"I've got to go," said Amy desperately. She wrenched her arm away from Lana's and began running a little wildly over the rocky beach. Her heart thumped heavily in her chest.

As she reached the clump of bushes, she paused and looked up just in time to see her aunt's flashlight disappear over the top of the ridge. She blinked her eyes and peered into the darkness, trying to pick out the path that ran up beside the cliff.

"This way," said a familiar voice beside her. It was Lana. Amy looked at her friend and saw a grim face outlined in silver by the full moon. "I can't let you go alone," Lana said quietly, her voice trembling. "This is my grandmother's Dreaming. Maybe together we'll be OK."

She looked Amy in the eye and drew her breath sharply. "Follow me," she said shortly and turned away.

Lana moved quickly and soundlessly up the narrow path. Amy followed as best she could, trying to ignore the pain of the sharp stones that tore at her bare feet. The path became steep and she found herself almost on all fours, scrambling up and up. A couple of times she stumbled, sending showers of small rocks cascading down behind her. It was hard work, and as they reached the top, Amy found she was gasping for breath. She could hear Lana beside her also breathing deeply. They stood together at the top of the rock face, looking down into the pool where they'd swum earlier that day. Beyond the water the car waited with its inside light burning dimly. Amy could almost make out the small huddled figures within.

"Come on," Lana urged, and they turned away from the cliff.

"Stop." Amy grabbed Lana's arm. "See if we can see Caroline's flashlight." She had not quite recovered her breath.

They stood for a moment, staring into the darkness. The landscape was scattered with rocky outcrops and huge boulders that caught the moonlight on their shoulders. Caroline could be anywhere. Amy wanted to call out for her aunt, but some deeper instinct stopped her and the cry stayed choked up in her chest.

"What's that?" Lana whispered beside her. Amy peered harder and then she saw it: away in the distance was a glow of light. It could be a flashlight—it could be Caroline.

Lana set off toward the light and Amy followed in silent agreement. But something was wrong. She felt it with a sinister certainty—that light glowing with a reddish tinge and so still, so absolutely still—beckoning them through the night.

The bright moonlight cast shadows in their path and Amy felt panic welling up in the pit of her stomach. She tried desperately to fight off her growing fear. But her senses were playing tricks on her and it seemed to her that the rocks were alive and watching them as they passed. Was that a boulder over there or a woman holding a baby in her arms? Was that a man, his black skin adorned with the white paint of ceremony?

Something touched her cheek with the caress of a hand and suddenly she broke into a run. She felt her hair pulled as she brushed past a boulder and laughter rang in her ears as loose strands of hair whipped around her face.

Now she ran, blind and stumbling, unaware of anything except the fear that engulfed her. All around the country was whispering, whispering—telling her its secrets.

"*No!*" something deep within her screamed, but no sound passed her lips. She fell to the ground and pressed her hands over her ears.

Voices, voices, voices. They were everywhere. Women's voices, speaking in tongues that she did not understand. Taunting, laughing, sobbing voices.

And then she heard her name. It came from far away, as though carried on the breeze. It was a voice that she knew—the dearest she had ever known. As it grew stronger, the other voices left, and Amy lifted her head again, searching the night with wild eyes.

"Mom!" her heart cried. "Oh, Mom. Don't leave me again. Take me with you."

But the stars winked at her and the shapes of the night moved closer. Amy bowed her head until her forehead brushed the earth, and closed her eyes tightly.

She lay very still and soon became conscious of a hand placed gently on her back. It was Lana crouched beside her. The girl was talking, almost singing, in a deep, soft voice—urgent words that seemed like an Aboriginal incantation.

Her voice made Amy sleepy. She sat up slowly, rubbing her eyes. And as she did, the ghosts left, vanishing as quickly as they'd come.

The night seemed to sigh with relief.

"It was my mother," whispered Amy.

Lana nodded slowly, her hand still on Amy's back.

"She's watching over you," she said quietly. "We'll be all right."

Amy turned questioning eyes toward her friend. "It really was her," she said again in wonder.

For a moment the girls sat still, staring up into the wide starry sky and feeling the light breeze on their skin. Amy brushed her hair off her face with one trembling hand. The band that had tied it back was gone, lying somewhere back among the rocks.

Amy sighed deeply. If only her father could be here, too. Or her aunt.

"Caroline. Oh, Caroline! Where are you?" she thought with sudden longing.

Her thoughts were interrupted by a sharp noise. Something or someone had dislodged a small stone just up ahead.

Amy wiped the back of her hand across her eyes and drew a deep breath. "Please let that be Caroline," she prayed.

She saw Lana creeping forward, crouched low to the ground. A moment later, the girl turned and motioned to Amy to follow. Amy took a deep breath and, mustering all her courage, followed her friend through the darkness.

A small outcrop of rock barred their way, and they could see that the red glow of light emanated from behind it. It was not from a flashlight. The girls could see that clearly now, and so they edged forward quietly and cautiously, unsure of what or who they might find.

It was easy to climb up the rocks, but Amy held her breath, hoping that no stone would be disturbed and clatter noisily to the ground. The surface was smooth and soon they were able to peek over the top of the outcrop.

Amy drew her breath sharply. So that was it. The light was coming from a lantern. A figure sat on the ground beside the light, but Amy was sure it was not her aunt. As they watched, the figure unfolded itself and turned so that the face was clearly illuminated in the lantern's rosy glow. It was Ricky!

Amy glanced at Lana, who returned her look with wide-eyed amazement. "*Kadaitcha wiya!*" Lana whispered. "This is no *kadaitcha!*"

Ricky was busy now. They could hear him mumbling to himself as he stood up and walked away a little. He knelt down and rummaged around in the rocks on the ground. What on earth was he doing? Amy strained to see, but the man had his back to them.

A moment later he turned, coming back with his strange, short-legged walk, over to the lantern. Amy could see that he had something in his hand. It looked as though it was quite heavy. A backpack with its neck gaping wide was propped up next to the lantern, and Ricky now placed the object deeply and carefully inside. He laughed sharply and Amy felt a shiver down her spine. Whatever this man was doing, he was up to no good.

"What's that in his hand?" she whispered in her friend's ear.

"I'm not sure," Lana whispered back. "It looks like a rock."

"It must have been the light from Ricky's lantern that scared Eddie at the camp," Amy whispered again. "He must have been checking who was at the water hole."

"Yeah, ugliest *kadaitcha* I've ever seen, that's for sure!" The girls smothered a nervous giggle behind their hands.

Suddenly they heard a noise over to one side, a stumble of uncertain feet. Amy looked around desperately but saw nothing. When she turned back, she saw Ricky standing, mouth open in surprise, for he had heard the noise as well. Then he hurried toward the open pack. A twist of his wrist at the lantern's neck, and then there was darkness.

"Come on," Lana urged at her shoulder. "That must have been Caroline. She must have found him, too."

Amy felt surprisingly calm as she carefully climbed back down from the rock. She knew now that to make a noise would be to give themselves away. Lana's shadowy shape was crouched low to the ground ahead of her. Slowly, slowly they crept along, keeping to the shadows and flattening their bodies against boulders.

Somewhere behind them came the sound of heavy boots. The man was walking slowly, trying to be silent, but he didn't belong to this country and was clumsy over the rocks. The girls heard him trip and swear under his breath. Then he was silent.

They moved on, wishing that the moon was not quite so bright. The sound of Ricky's heavy boots had stopped.

"What's he doing?" thought Amy. Somehow it had been less frightening when they could hear the trudge of his boots.

"Stop," hissed Lana, laying an arm on Amy's shoulder. She leaned forward until her mouth was close to Amy's ear and whispered as softly as she could, "I think he might be up ahead. I heard something, but I'm not sure how he got there so quickly. We'll have to double back a little."

"Do you think he's working with someone else?" Amy whispered back, just as quietly.

"Could be," Lana replied, and turned back the way they'd come.

They crept quickly and quietly back for a minute and then turned so that they were again traveling toward the top of the rock face above the water hole. Amy could hardly wait to reach the safety of the camp and wished now that they'd never left. They could have been sitting in the back of the car, huddled up with the other children, or even on their way back to the town. Amy wished that she hadn't acted so rashly, and yet Caroline was still up here somewhere—but where?

Amy felt a twist in her heart and stopped to look back over her shoulder. As she did, she tripped and fell, crashing to the ground.

"Amy!" Lana stopped and knelt beside her, but it was too late.

"Stop!" a deep voice ordered and they were suddenly caught in a beam of light. Amy blinked and shielded her eyes. The man was a shadow behind the glare of his flashlight, but the girls knew with certainty that it was Ricky.

"Well, well, well, what have we here?" he jeered, coming closer. "Just out for a midnight stroll, are we?"

As he neared, Lana grabbed Amy and dragged her up to her feet, where she swayed a little. It seemed as though her legs were made of jelly.

Ricky was glaring at Lana. "Might have known that you'd be mixed up in this," he said and waved a stick menacingly toward her.

He took another couple of steps toward them and Amy saw that he had bare feet. So that was how he'd managed to walk so quietly—he'd taken his heavy boots off.

She could see his face now, twisted and ugly with hate. He waved the stick again and this time Amy saw it glint in the beam of the flashlight. A moment later she realized that Ricky had a rifle and watched in horror as he lowered it, pointing the barrel straight at Lana. Amy felt numb with fear.

It was then that Amy saw her aunt step out of the darkness.

"Leave them alone," Caroline ordered. "Pick on someone your own size."

Ricky put his head back and laughed; not a jovial laugh but a forced evil bray through crooked teeth. "My goodness," he said, his voice heavy with scorn. "How many of you are out here? You've all caused me a lot of trouble tonight."

Caroline walked over to the girls and put an arm

around each protectively. "Listen," she said in a quiet voice. "Why don't you just go. I've seen what you're up to—stealing Aboriginal sacred objects from a sacred site. I'm sure you'll sell them for a small fortune in the big cities. Now just take your things and go. Don't make this worse for yourself. Get a head start and go now."

Ricky laughed again. "Oh yes. But what about you, eh? You'll go straight back down to town and the police, won't you? Turning poor little Ricky in. No, I'll need a really good head start and I think I know just how to organize that."

"Yes," he said slowly, and his eyes became those of a madman. "Move over there!" He gestured with the gun at Lana again. "I'm going to slow you down a bit, all right."

"Come on," he yelled at Lana. He rested his flashlight on a rock and grabbed the rifle in both hands. Lana seemed uncertain and Amy knew that she must be feeling the same dreamlike daze that dampened her senses. Like a sleepwalker, Lana began to move.

"This is . . ." began Caroline, but was cut short by a string of obscenities.

"Get over there," he said again to Lana. And then a change seemed to come over Lana. She stood up tall and put her shoulders back. She walked a few steps and turned with defiance to face the man. There was almost a smile on her lips as she looked at him with disdain.

"The spirits will get you, blue eyes," she said quietly. "You can't harm me here. This is my grandmother's Dreaming."

Ricky lifted the rifle and pointed it straight at the girl. "You don't frighten me," he said, his shoulders heaving with emotion. "I've had enough of you Abos with your primitive ways and your stupid stories. You make me sick."

It all happened so quickly. Amy's mind whirred into a blank as the rifle went off. The noise echoed in her ears and she felt a body fall heavily against her, knocking her to the ground. There was a crack as a head hit the hard ground and then silence. It was suddenly very dark.

How long she lay there, it was hard to say. Slowly the haze of terror cleared and she became aware of something resting on the ground in front of her face. It was Caroline's flashlight. She reached for it and turned it on. The batteries must have been nearly dead, since the beam was a dim sickly yellow. Amy pulled herself up and looked around. Ricky had disappeared and there was no sign of Lana. Beside her on the ground lay her aunt, very still and silent. A dark stain was seeping through Caroline's tracksuit pants. Amy touched it and felt the blood still warm from her aunt's body.

"You're bleeding," Amy whimpered and drew back in alarm. There was no reply and Amy brought the torch up next to Caroline's face. Her aunt lay with her eyes closed, her head resting by the rock onto which she had fallen. Her mouth was open and she was still breathing.

"Thank goodness for that," Amy thought. "But what do I do now? Oh, Caroline, I don't know what to do." She suddenly felt very cold. Her teeth began to chatter and she began to shake very slightly.

"Come on, come on," she said out loud to herself. "Stay calm, Amy. Stay calm. Come on, you can do it." It was the sort of thing her mother would have said to her. She began to think. What about that first aid course they'd done last year at school. Bleeding. What was it you were supposed to do for bleeding? Pressure. Yes, that was it. Apply a pressure bandage.

She looked around for something she could use as a bandage and then at her own light tracksuit top. Yes, that would do. Quickly she stripped down to her T-shirt and with trembling hands balanced the flashlight on a rock to free her hands. The stain on Caroline's pants was now quite large and Amy gingerly peeled back the wet cloth from her aunt's skin to reveal the bullet wound at the top of her leg. She folded her own tracksuit top until it was a thick wad of material and applied it firmly over the bleeding. "Good," she thought. "That's good. But what next?"

"Amy! Amy!" a voice called. It was Lana.

"Over here," Amy cried. "Over here." She picked up the flashlight and waved it above her head.

A moment later Lana appeared, with Barbara close behind. The blonde-haired health worker knelt down beside Caroline and took her pulse. Then she gently lifted both of Caroline's eyelids and shone a light briefly into each eye.

"Is she all right?" Amy heard herself ask. Her voice sounded strange, high and tight.

"*Yuwa*," Barbara answered. "But we must get her to the hospital." She shook her head and added in a shaking voice: "I knew that there would be problems if we broke the law and came up here."

"Will you be all right?" Lana asked, looking anxiously about.

"Yes," replied Barbara softly. "I'm sure it will be understood that in this situation there was no choice. Caroline needs help. She's lost a lot of blood."

"I put this here to try and stop the bleeding," said Amy.

"It's good," replied Barbara. "You did well."

Amy felt tears well up in her eyes and then spill down her cheeks in relief as a dozen different emotions cascaded over her exhausted mind.

"That bullet was meant for me." Lana spoke softly in the dark. "He meant to shoot me."

"Well, he's a lousy shot as well as a lousy store manager," said Barbara.

"*Wiya*—no," Lana said slowly. "Caroline pushed me out of the way. He'd have got me fair and square if she hadn't thrown herself at me to get me out of the way. She saved my life," she added thickly.

The three sat for a moment as the impact of Lana's words sank in.

"Come on," said Barbara, clearing her throat. "It's our turn to save her now. Listen, I'll stay here with her. Lana, I know that you can drive. Take these keys and go to Jack for help. He'll know what to do. Quickly, now, both of you—go!"

She looked up at the two girls standing quietly, looking at the limp form of Caroline's body on the ground.

"*Go!*" she said again.

Amy stooped and picked up her aunt's hand. She held it briefly, then placed it gently back down on the cool ground. "Yes," she said, turning to Lana. "Let's go."

10
A Drive in the Dark

"I thought you said you could drive," said Amy accusingly to her friend as the car bunny-hopped down the track back into the town.

"Well, we've gotten here haven't we?" Lana countered, obviously very proud of herself. She stood on the clutch and wrestled to change gear. Clunk! The car leaped forward as Lana jumped back onto the pile of pillows she needed to see over the dashboard, steadying the steering wheel with both hands.

Amy had to admit it—they had gotten back, although there had been times as they'd jolted and stalled over the rough dirt road that she'd wondered if they would. But Lana had done it, and now the glow of the few streetlights welcomed them into the quietness of the sleeping town.

"We're here," Amy said over her shoulder to the children who had remained wide-eyed and silent in the back. One little one began to whimper.

Lana slowed down and then, holding the wheel tight, jumped down onto the brake with all her strength. She hadn't meant to stop the car with such force. Amy was catapulted into the dashboard.

"Thanks a lot," she said, rubbing her nose and frowning.

"Sorry," said Lana, hauling the hand brake on and sitting up again. She turned to the children who were picking themselves up off the floor of the vehicle. "Here you go, kids. You stay at the single women's camp tonight. They'll look after you."

The small children didn't need persuading. Soon they were tumbling out of the back doors into the loving arms of the women of the camp. A few words were exchanged and then Lana climbed back up into the driver's seat.

"Can't we find someone else to drive," moaned Amy, but Lana didn't answer. She was too busy finding the right gear and in a minute they bounced forward and the car rattled once more off down the road.

"Now," said Lana with determination, "Jack's place."

Her uncle's place turned out to be on the outskirts of the town. It was a small neat house that shone white in the moonlight. Jack's blue pickup was parked in the driveway.

"I'll wait in the car," said Amy, thinking back to the hateful look that Jack had given her when they'd last met.

"No, no," insisted Lana. "You must come in. Come on."

Amy sighed and climbed down. Her legs felt a little funny as they stepped down onto the sand. She felt like she'd just run a marathon that had left her muscles weak and trembling with fatigue.

The house door stood wide open, and as they neared, Amy could see Jack quite clearly. He was sitting reading a newspaper, feet crossed up on the table in front of him, a coffee mug by one elbow.

"Jack, Jack!" Lana called breathlessly, breaking into a run. Amy saw him start and he wheeled around, still holding the paper in one hand.

"What is it, Nangala?" he asked anxiously.

Lana ran in and flung her arms around her bewildered uncle.

"It's Caroline. She's been shot." There was no reply, so she continued, stepping back and looking anxiously into her uncle's face.

"We surprised Ricky up above the water hole and he had a gun . . . and . . . and . . ." Lana stopped as she watched the expression changing on Jack's face. She took a step back, amazed and horrified.

"So, you want me to come and help some poor whitefella?" he asked, his face bitter and his eyes cold. He shook his head. "Nangala, Nangala, haven't you been listening to anything I've told you over the years? So," he laughed shortly and turned away, "they've started shooting each other now, have they?" He picked up his paper, which had fallen to the floor.

"But Jack!" Lana persisted, "Caroline has been our friend. She's come to our town because she wants to learn and to help."

Jack interrupted his niece angrily. "You don't know what you're talking about, girl. Caroline is here for her own good, that's all. Wants to buy a place in heaven, or maybe get a few research papers written on the poor blackfella."

He sat down again and his eyes narrowed. "You watch—soon she'll leave, having had her 'Aboriginal experience' and go back to the city. She'll be right for dinner party stories for years—making fun of our ways and culture and feeling sorry for us." He shook his head once more and then noticed Amy, who was standing quietly in the shadows just outside the door.

"And I see you've still got your whitefella friend. Go on, get out of here—both of you. Out!" He turned his back to them both and opened his paper decisively.

Lana stood frozen with emotion, then at last turned slowly and walked, eyes down, toward the door.

"Come on," she said. "That stuck-up pig's no good to us. I hope I never have to see him again!" She spoke loudly, hoping that Jack had heard, and Amy glanced nervously at the figure still sitting at the table, half expecting him to react violently to Lana's taunting words. But he didn't move and she breathed a silent sigh of relief.

"OK," Lana said, wiping a quiet tear from her eye and sniffing a little. "To the police station next."

She started the ignition and Amy gripped the seat with both hands, anticipating the jolt forward.

A short time later, they sat in the car outside the police station with the engine humming, staring blankly into the night.

"What now?" asked Lana with a helpless sigh.

"Well," Amy said slowly, "the policeman's wife said they'd be back in about an hour. She said she'd radio their car right away." Amy shook her head in disbelief. She couldn't believe their bad luck. The police, the remaining nurse, Elizabeth, and the health workers had all been called to another emergency in a nearby camp.

Amy thought of her aunt lying quiet and bleeding, and knew that to wait an hour was not possible. No, they'd just have to manage alone.

"Let's go to the clinic," she said. "We might be able to find some bandages or something."

Amy thought back to the night when Caroline had rushed off to help Lana's grandmother. "Yes, we could get the red emergency box," she said, trying to sound enthusiastic. But it was far from how she really felt. As the car bumped on, she looked around at the town that she had begun to know. Now it had changed back into a dangerous stranger. She felt oddly detached, as though she were watching herself act out a part in a play, and the cold of the desert night began to prickle the skin of her bare arms.

The clinic building stood dark and silent, a black solid square.

"No one here," Lana murmured as she opened the car door. "I suppose we should get the emergency box and then see if we can find some people to help us."

The key ring Barbara had given them had four keys attached. A streetlight nearby cast enough light to locate the lock and soon the right key slid into the keyhole and the girls pushed the door open. Lana fumbled for a switch and a moment later a comforting yellow light flooded the building. Amy suddenly felt a little more optimistic.

"The box is over here, I think," she said as she turned into the storeroom. She remembered having seen Caroline put it there and was relieved to see she was right.

"Lana," she called.

"I'm here. Just getting some bandages," came her friend's voice from another room.

Amy looked around. Was there anything else they might need?

She walked into the main clinic room and opened a few cupboard doors. She found some new batteries that would be useful for the flashlight and then went to find Lana. As she passed the radio room, she stopped and turned. Then she put her hand to her head.

"The radio," she said out loud. "Of course . . . Lana!"

Lana appeared with an armful of bandages, looking a little alarmed. "What's the matter?" she asked.

"I don't know why I didn't think of it before."

"Think of what?" asked Lana. But then she saw the radio and understood what Amy meant. She thought for a moment and then her face fell. "But I don't know how to use it. Someone else has always done it." Her voice trailed off as she walked up to the radio that sat silent and still along the bench.

"Caroline showed me once," said Amy. She frowned with concentration. A switch on one side of the radio had "On/Off" marked clearly beside it.

"What do you think?" asked Amy.

"Might as well try."

Lana flicked the switch and was rewarded with a crackle and a couple of red lights that stared at them unwinking.

"I'm sure it's this red button you hold down in an emergency to get the radio person in Alice Springs to answer," said Amy. "I'm sure that's what Caroline said."

"Yes," said Lana. "I think that's what I've seen them do. You're closer. Do you want to push it?"

"OK." Amy nodded and pushed the red button firmly, holding it depressed with one trembling finger. She closed her eyes. "Please, please, let someone be there. Let someone hear." Silence.

Then a crackle of static.

"VJD, this is VJD. Do you read me?" The radio spoke. The reception was good and the voice clear.

"Yes, yes," Amy cried and snatched up the microphone. "Yes, um . . . this is Victor, Mike . . . Six . . . um." Amy looked up and saw the call sign printed along the top of the radio set. She took a deep breath and started again.

"This is Victor Mike Six Romeo Yankee. Please help us. We need help."

There was a pause that seemed like hours, then the voice crackled again.

"Victor Mike Six Romeo Yankee. We read you loud and clear," said a woman's voice and Amy could have cried for joy.

"What's the problem? Over," said the voice.

"There's been a shooting. Caroline Wilson, the nurse, has been shot in the leg and she's unconscious . . . and it happened outside town at the water hole . . . Um . . . Over."

"Message understood," came the voice. "Who am I talking to? Over."

"This is Amy Wilson, Caroline's niece, and Lana Nangala is here, too. Over."

"OK. Now listen, Amy. Is Elizabeth there? Over."

"No, she's at another emergency and the police are there, too. Over."

The radio was silent for a moment and then at last the voice spoke again. "Amy, do you read me? Over."

"Yes . . . Over."

"I will arrange for an ambulance to come out right away. I believe the airstrip is not safe for night flights at the moment so we can't send the Flying Doctor. The ambulance will get there in about two hours. In the meantime, try to get Caroline into town, get some help. Take an oxygen cylinder with you, if you can find one, and some bandages. Have you got that? Over."

"Yes, I have. Barbara, the health worker, is with her now. Over," Amy said, starting to feel a little more hopeful.

"She's in good hands then," the voice continued. "All right, I'll organize the ambulance. Call back if there are any further problems. We'll be standing by. Is there anything else? Over."

"No," said Amy and then looked at Lana who shook her head. "No. Over."

"OK, then. Over and out." The voice left them and all of a sudden it was just Amy and Lana standing alone in the middle of the empty building. The radio static crackled away in the background.

Lana turned to her friend. "We did it," she said triumphantly.

"*Yuwa*," Amy agreed, and smiled as she realized she'd used an Aboriginal word without thinking. Then she sighed as her thoughts turned to the daunting task that lay before them. She looked around. "Do you know where the oxygen cylinder is?" she asked her friend.

Lana didn't know, but they soon found it. The cylinder was very heavy and the two girls lugged it out of the clinic, swaying a little with the effort. Amy stretched her fingers out in relief as they put the cylinder down for a minute while Lana relocked the clinic door.

As they went to pick it up once again, a deep, gruff voice sounded behind them. "Here, I'll help you with that."

"Jack!" Lana said in a voice tinged with disbelief.

"Yes, I know. Come on. You've wasted enough time already," he grumbled as he heaved the oxygen cylinder into the back of the car.

Lana jumped up into the front seat, a look of wonder on her face, but Amy hung back, unsure. Jack turned and looked her directly in the eye. "It's OK," he said with surprising gentleness. "Get in."

Silently she obeyed and climbed up next to Lana, who gave her hand a quick squeeze of reassurance.

"What midget's been driving this car?" asked Jack as he threw all the pillows over into the back.

"I wouldn't call it driving," Amy ventured and Jack laughed.

"Leave me alone," Lana protested and gave her friend a gentle nudge in the ribs.

"You called an ambulance?" Jack asked shortly.

"Yes," said Lana. "We tried to get the police, but they weren't there."

"I know. I called in at the police station, too."

The car picked up speed and they left the dim glow of the town's streetlights behind them.

Amy began to think about what they might find at the water hole. "Please be all right, Caroline," she prayed to herself. "Please . . . please."

"Now, Nangala. Tell me exactly what happened," Jack was saying. "I want all the details."

"Well . . ." Lana began, and Amy listened as the story was related, half in English and half in Luritja.

11
Rescue

"Jack, Jack! Over here." Barbara's voice sounded ahead in the dark.

"Auntie," Lana called and swung her torch in a wide arc in front of her. Amy and Jack followed over the rocky track.

"Here," Barbara called again, and as she did, the flashlight caught her figure waving at them a short distance ahead.

"Thank goodness," thought Amy, as they hurried forward. She drew a deep breath. Her side was beginning to ache with the effort and she felt quite exhausted. They had run practically all the way from the water hole, up the narrow path and over the expanse of rocky plateau.

"How is she?" she panted, collapsing onto the rocks beside her aunt.

"Her pulse is very weak," replied Barbara. "She's still unconscious. We need to get her to the hospital."

Amy held her aunt's hand gently between her own. It felt very cold.

"Is it safe to move her?" asked Jack gruffly as he placed the oxygen cylinder down on the ground with care.

"We've got no choice." Barbara shone the flashlight on Caroline's face and Amy felt a small shiver travel all the way down her spine. Her aunt looked so pale and helpless. Amy closed her eyes thinking, "Please, please, don't die. Just this once make Old Ruby be wrong about someone dying. Please."

Barbara gently placed the oxygen mask over Caroline's face and then busied herself replacing the bandage that was now soaked with the red stain of blood.

Jack knelt down beside Caroline and shook his head. "I hope the police get that idiot, Ricky. If they don't, I will." He looked up at Barbara. "The girls told me what happened. You know that she saved Lana?"

"Yes, I know," said Barbara in a very quiet, low voice.

Jack slipped one arm under Caroline's neck and the other under her knees.

"Careful with that oxygen line," cautioned Barbara.

"OK." Jack braced his back and lifted Caroline's limp form.

"Now keep that flashlight steady on the ground in front of me, Lana," Jack ordered. "I don't want to trip on these rocks."

It was difficult enough walking on the flat rock plateau, but when they traversed the steep track that led down beside the water hole, Jack slipped several times, sending showers of small rocks flying. Barbara followed closely with the oxygen cylinder weighing heavily on one arm. Lana and Amy had the flashlights and tried their very best to keep the path lit for the others with their precious load.

At last they were at the car. Amy climbed into the back with Barbara and helped arrange several blankets and pillows on the floor between the seats. When they'd finished, Jack laid Caroline gently down on the rough bed. The dim light on the car ceiling glowed above them.

"All right, we'll put the oxygen cylinder here," said Barbara, and then noticed the emergency box. "Good for you." She smiled at Amy.

Barbara flicked back the lid of the box and rustled around for a minute. "Now, Lana," she said at last. "Hold the flashlight right here on Caroline's arm. We're going to give her some fluid into a vein to make up for the blood loss. Amy," she added, "could you please hold this." She handed Amy a small reel of white tape. "Break some small pieces off and hand them to me when I ask for them. *Palya?*"

Amy watched, holding her breath, as Barbara inserted a large needle into her aunt's arm. With everyone concentrating hard, it was so quiet that she could hear the soft hiss of the oxygen as it made its way from the cylinder through the tubing and into the mask that covered Caroline's nose and mouth.

"Tape!" Amy jumped and handed Barbara a small length of tape, which was applied firmly to keep the needle in place. Several more pieces of tape followed until the health worker was satisfied that the intravenous line was quite secure. Soon clear fluid was running from a large plastic bag through another clear plastic tube into Caroline's arm.

"That will help replace the blood," Barbara explained. "I'll just check her blood pressure again. Amy, can you hold this bag of fluid up as high as you can and tell me when it gets close to empty? We'll have to hold it up like that all the way to town, so tell me when your arm gets sore and then Lana can take a turn."

"No problem," said Amy, glad to be feeling useful and feeling more hopeful.

"We may as well take her as far as we can toward Alice Springs and meet the ambulance on the road," Jack suggested from where he stood at the back of the car. He sounded very tired but determined.

Barbara nodded in reply. "Blood pressure's getting better. I think we're OK to go."

Amy's arm had already begun to ache. The bag of fluid was surprisingly heavy. She was relieved when Barbara took it from her. Jack walked around and climbed up into the driver's seat.

"I'll have to take it a little easy over this rough road," he said. "We can speed up once we're onto the main road."

Amy sat in the back next to her aunt's unconscious form.

"Can I hold her hand?" she asked Barbara, who nodded with a gentle smile.

Amy was surprised how cold and lifeless Caroline's hand felt. She wrapped her warm fingers around it and held tight. There seemed for a moment to be a flicker of response in her aunt's fingers, but then nothing. The hand sat limp within Amy's own.

Just outside the town they saw another vehicle coming toward them. The headlights were at first just a dim glow ahead in the dark, but as they approached, the glow separated into two distinct beams, bouncing over the rough road. At first she thought it was the ambulance, but it soon became apparent that it was the police vehicle instead.

Jack pulled up at the side of the road and got out, waving the other car down. It stopped and the police officer met Jack in the middle of the road. After a brief discussion, they came over and opened the back of the car.

"Sorry I wasn't around to help," the police officer said apologetically. "It's been quite a night. Elizabeth's on her way back to town. Should be here soon." He looked at Caroline and then questioningly at Barbara. "She'll be all right?" he asked.

"*Yuwa*, Mike. Yes, I think so," replied Barbara. "But the sooner we get her to the hospital, the better."

"Right, I'll let you go then," said the police officer, stepping back. "But I thought you might like to know that we picked Ricky up. He's in the lock-up right now."

"Did he put up much of a fight?" asked Jack.

"No," said the policeman and gave a short puzzled laugh. "Not at all. It's kind of strange, actually. We found him crawling along the ground just out of town like he was drunk. Couldn't get any sense out of him. He kept saying something about ghosts, or demons, or something up in the hills that was out to get him. He was terrified."

Amy saw Lana and Barbara exchange a look. "They know something," Amy thought to herself.

"We found a backpack nearby," the police officer continued. "It was full of strange shaped rocks. One of the old women has confirmed that they are sacred objects used in ceremonies—probably thousands of years old. I'll bet that old Ricky meant to sell them. They'd be worth a lot of money."

Barbara knelt and took Caroline's blood pressure again and the police officer cleared his throat. "Well, I'd better let you people get on your way. I'll radio the ambulance and tell them you're coming."

It was hard to tell how long they'd been traveling before they saw the red flashing lights of the ambulance approaching them down the road. The two vehicles stopped, out on the sandy plain so far from anywhere, and Caroline was transferred onto a stretcher and then into the ambulance by two competent aides in white uniforms. Amy held her aunt's hand the whole time, but eventually it was time for the ambulance to close its doors and get on its way. She felt Jack's hand on her shoulder.

"Come on, Amy. We have to leave now, but we'll all go into Alice Springs tomorrow. We can radio the hospital first thing in the morning."

Amy nodded, tears starting in her eyes. She felt more exhausted than she had ever felt before in her life and her fingers didn't seem to want to let go of Caroline's cold hand. It was as though they had a mind of their own.

"Come on," said Jack again, gently.

"Good-bye, Caroline," Amy whispered close to her aunt's ear. Then she slowly untwined her fingers.

Amy and Lana sat in the back of the car and watched the lights of the ambulance disappearing down the road. Amy gave a sigh. She was so very, very tired.

The sky had taken on the pale sheen of dawn, the color of a pink cockatoo in flight. The scrub on either side of the road began to emerge from the shadows.

Amy felt her eyes closing but she was soon jolted awake by a rough patch of road. The trip back to the settlement was a blur in the numbness of her weary brain. She did register the buildings as they drove into town and was soon aware of Jack lifting Lana and then herself out of the car. She was carried into a house and soon felt the welcome softness of a mattress beneath her aching body and knew that Lana was there beside her.

"It's daylight," she thought in a hazy sort of way as sleep took over at last.

12
Melbourne

Amy sat at her desk in her bedroom, gazing out the window into the suburbs of Melbourne. Her black cowboy hat rested by her elbow, a reminder that her recent adventures in Central Australia had been real.

She was distracted from her thoughts momentarily when she saw the next-door neighbors arriving home: the Fullers with their big expensive cars, their mansion, and their vacation home in the countryside. Yes, the Fullers were the perfect family—glamorous mother, important father, and two angelic children—or rather, that's what Amy used to think. Now suddenly she realized that she'd changed. She wasn't jealous anymore.

"I bet they've never camped by a water hole in the middle of the desert," she thought, "or been told Dreamtime stories by an old Aboriginal woman."

"I wonder if old Mrs. Crippen down the road has any stories to tell," she mused. "She might remember some stories of the olden days, even if she can't get my name right!"

Her thoughts were interrupted by a sound from the bedroom door.

"Amy, can we come in?" It was her father. As he pushed the door open, Amy saw that Emma was with him.

"How are you now? Still tired?" he asked, laying a hand on her shoulder. "You've been awfully quiet lately."

"Just thinking, Dad," smiled Amy. "I've had a lot to think about."

"Your dad told me about what happened on your trip," said Emma in her usual quiet way. "It must have been quite an experience."

"Yes," said Amy shortly. It had become a habit to answer any of Emma's questions with the minimal number of words. She had put up barriers long ago that were meant to be impenetrable even to this gentle woman's kindness. No one could replace her mother. But now she felt her defenses give just a little. She looked at Emma and saw that she was feeling hurt, snubbed, and uncomfortable. She'd lowered her eyes and her face was flushed pink.

"I think I'd better be going, Robert," Emma said.

Only a month ago, Amy would have viewed this as a small triumph, but now—well, it didn't feel good at all. She saw the hurt and disappointment on her father's face and made up her mind.

"No," Amy said, getting up. "Don't go." She saw the look on their faces change to surprise and almost disbelief.

"Well, I really don't know," Emma stammered, looking from Robert to Amy and then back again.

"I'd like to tell you about Central Australia." Amy managed to force the words out, wondering how she would start to describe what she'd been through.

"I would really like to hear about it," ventured Emma cautiously. "I spent some time in Central Australia working as a teacher."

"Really?" Amy felt genuinely enthusiastic. "Then you would understand what it was like."

"Maybe a little, but it was a long time ago." Emma seemed lost in thought for a moment and Amy's father took advantage of the pause to toss a letter onto Amy's desk.

"Thought you might like this. It just came," he said with a smile. "We'll leave you in peace. Come downstairs when you're ready. Maybe we can all go for a walk on the beach."

When Amy was alone she studied the envelope closely. It was addressed to "Miss A. Wilson" and the postage mark said "ALICE SPRINGS" in a circle of slightly smudged ink. She turned it over. No sender, but that didn't matter. She knew who it was from.

Amy teased the envelope open and drew out the folded paper. Carefully she spread the letter in front of her, smoothing out the creases with her fingers.

Dear Amy,

Well, I'm back at school and I guess that you are, too. It's not so bad I suppose, but I'd rather be swimming in the water hole.

I'm staying with my auntie (yes— ANOTHER auntie) in Alice Springs again and Uncle Jack is visiting at the moment. In fact, he's stayed quite a while. Do you want to hear something really amazing? Are you sure??? OK! Get ready for it. Jack took Caroline to see a movie on Tuesday night. He said that he was just doing her a favor—you know, with Caroline having to be in a wheelchair for a month or so.

Things seem to be going well for Jack now. He got a job at one of the schools. Thinks he might save some money and go on to college or something. He's always on about this education business. Can't understand it myself.

What else can I tell you? Oh yes. Ricky is still in jail. They found out that he'd been stealing money from the store as well as dealing in stolen sacred objects and paintings. Apparently he already had a lot of money stashed away.

Also, I've got some sad news. You'll remember how my grandmother said that someone would die. Well she was right—but she was talking about herself. She died in her sleep last week. I feel really strange about it all. I should explain that when an Aboriginal person dies, you aren't allowed to speak or write their name. Anyone with the same name is called Kwementyaye (you say that as Koo-man-jai, roughly). You aren't even allowed to have any photos or videos of the dead person. Everyone has moved away from the place where she lived and soon they'll smoke the wiltja and have ceremonies. My grandmother was an important lady. I miss her a lot. I didn't ask you if you had any grandparents. Please write and tell me if you have and all about them.

I miss you, too. Caroline says that when she goes to Melbourne for Christmas, she might take me, too. I think that would be great. I've never seen a big city. You could show me around and maybe we could go to see a movie or something.

Anyway, in the meantime, I'll just write you letters, but only if you write back.

Love,
Lana (Nangala—your skin sister!)